Sophie Flakes Out

Other books in the growing Faithgirlz!™ library

TNIV Best Friends Bible
NIV Faithgirlz! Backpack Bible
My Faithgirlz! Journal

The Sophie Series
Sophie's World (Book One)
Sophie's Secret (Book Two)
Sophie and the Scoundrels (Book Three)
Sophie's Irish Showdown (Book Four)
Sophie's First Dance? (Book Five)
Sophie's Stormy Summer (Book Six)
Sophie Breaks the Code (Book Seven)
Sophie Tracks a Thief (Book Eight)
Sophie Loves Jimmy (Book Ten)
Sophie Loses the Lead (Book Eleven)
Sophie's Encore (Book Twelve)

Nonfiction

No Boys Allowed: Devotions for Girls
Girlz Rock: Devotions for You
Chick Chat: More Devotions for Girls

Check out www.faithgirlz.com

faiThGirLz!™

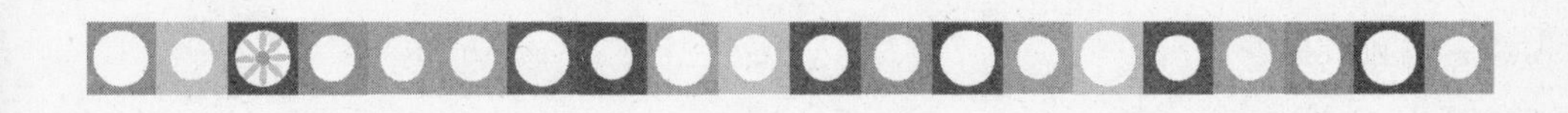

Sophie Flakes Out

Nancy Rue

zonderkidz

www.zonderkidz.com

Sophie Flakes Out

Requests for information should be addressed to:
Zonderkidz, 5300 Patterson Ave. SE
Grand Rapids, Michigan 49530

Library of Congress Cataloging-in-Publication Data

Rue, Nancy N.
Sophie flakes out / Nancy Rue.
p. cm.–(Faithgirlz)
Summary: Seventh-grader Sophie asks Jesus for guidance in dealing with her overprotective parents, her troubled friend, Willoughby, and a difficult Film Club project.
ISBN 10: 0-310-71024-3 (softcover)
ISBN 13: 978-0-310-71024-0 (softcover)
[1. Parent and child—Fiction. 2. Christian life—Fiction. 3. Conduct of life—Fiction. 4. Middle schools—Fiction. 5. Schools—Fiction.] I. Title. II. Series.
PZ7.R88515Sjk 2006
[Fic]–dc22
2005016638

Published in association with the literary agency of Alive Communications, Inc., 7680 Goddard Street, Suite 200, Colorado Springs, CO 80920.

Photography: Synergy Photographic/Brad Lampe
Illustrations: Grace Chen Design & Illustration
Art direction/design: Merit Alderink
Interior design: Susan Ambs
Interior composition: Ruth Bandstra

Printed in the United States of America

06 07 08 09 10 • 8 7 6 5 4 3 2 1

So we fix our eyes not on what is seen, but on what is unseen.
For what is seen is temporary, but what is unseen is eternal.

— 2 Corinthians 4:18

1

"Dad-dy!" Sophie LaCroix closed her brown eyes behind her glasses so she wouldn't narrow them at her father or, worse, roll them at him. Daddy didn't like eye-rolling.

"Look, Soph," Daddy said. "I can't break it down for you any further. The answer is no. End of discussion."

Sophie wailed anyway, pipsqueak voice rising to the kitchen ceiling. "I'll be the only one in the whole entire *school* who doesn't get to see the movie."

Daddy squinted at her as he shrugged into his black NASA jacket. He didn't like whining either. "I'm sure there are other parents who don't want their twelve-year-olds seeing a PG–13 movie about gangs."

"It's a documentary!" Sophie said. "It's about real life."

Daddy's dark eyebrows shot up. "That makes it okay?" He picked up his laptop case and ran his other hand down the back of his spiky hair. "Drive-by shootings and foul language are not a part of *your* real life, and I'd like to keep it that way."

"What do I tell Mrs. Clayton and Ms. Hess?"

"Tell them I'll be calling your principal with a full explanation."

When Sophie opened her mouth, Daddy closed it with a black look. He didn't like arguing more than he didn't like anything.

He's calling Mr. Bentley? Sophie thought as she hoisted her backpack over her shoulder. *That is the most humiliating thing I can think of.*

It was probably worse than humiliating. She'd have to ask her best friend Fiona Bunting, the walking dictionary, for a word to describe feeling like a kindergartner in a seventh-grade body.

"Don't forget, it's your day to watch Zeke after school," Daddy said from the doorway. "Walk you to the bus stop, Baby Girl?"

How about NO! Sophie wanted to shriek. But she didn't even want to find out how much Daddy didn't like shrieking.

As she trudged to the corner, Sophie felt as if she had a chain attached to her ankle, and for somebody as small a twelve-year-old as she was, that was not a good thing. She could almost imagine it clanking on the sidewalk. But, then, she could imagine almost anything.

But I don't have to imagine how heinous this *situation is!* she told herself. It wasn't just having to babysit her six-year-old brother while her mom, who was going to have LaCroix Kid Number Four in a few months, cooked dinner. Zeke wasn't even that bad since he'd figured out New Baby Girl wasn't going to wipe out life as he knew it. And it wasn't just that Daddy wouldn't let her go to the movie that everybody in the entire school was seeing that day—except her.

It's just all of it, Sophie thought.

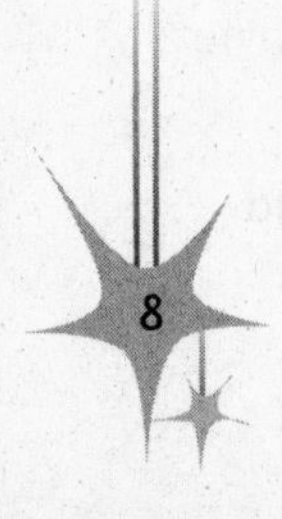

She climbed aboard the bus and slumped into her usual seat behind Harley and Gill, the two soccer-playing girls Sophie and her friends (the Corn Flakes) referred to as the Wheaties.

"Hi, you guys," she said.

But they only nodded at her vaguely. Their eyes were glued to the other side of the bus, a few rows back.

"Dude," Gill said, her green eyes wide. "Cell phones?" She shook her head so that two lanky tendrils of reddish hair fell out from under her wool, billed cap.

As usual, husky Harley just grunted.

Sophie swiveled around to catch sight of two girls sitting on the reserved-for-eighth-graders-only side. The very blonde one with even blonder highlights had a phone pressed to her ear, and her striking blue eyes were dancing a reply to the person on the other end. She pulled her hair up in a handful and let it fall like a fountain of blondeness to her shoulders as she laughed.

"It's only eight o'clock in the morning," Sophie whispered. "Who could she be talking to?"

"Probably the girl next to her," Gill said.

The talker's seatmate was a slender girl with a wispy cut to her honey brown hair that made her look like a stylish elf. Her lips were moving, but she seemed to be chatting to nobody.

"Where's her phone?" Sophie said to Gill.

"In her ear," Gill said. "See the wire coming down?"

Just then the girl glanced their way, and Gill and Harley turned in their seats like they were about to be shot. But although there was an unspoken rule that seventh graders didn't stare at eighth graders, just like they didn't even venture into the eighth-grade halls, Sophie couldn't pull her eyes from the girl's golden brown ones as she raised her teen-magazine eyebrows at Sophie. Even though they'd been riding the same bus for three months, it was the first time

she seemed to notice Sophie. Being seen by a girl who looked so together was like being under a spell.

The girl spread out her palms as if to say, "Well?"

"Sorry," Sophie said. She shriveled back into her seventh-grade world.

"I can't believe they're taking cell phones to school," Gill whispered over the back of the seat.

"I'll never even own one 'til I'm out of college or something," Sophie whispered back. Even her fourteen-year-old sister, Lacie, didn't have one, and she was in high school.

Sophie scooted closer to the bus window and gazed out through her glasses as Poquoson, Virginia, went by in a November mist. *I'll never even get a phone in my* room, she thought. *My conversations with my friends might as well be on the six o'clock news.*

Not to mention the whole rest of her life. In less than an hour, everybody in her section at school would know that her parents didn't think she could handle a PG–13 movie.

They're way overprotective, Sophie thought. And then she squirmed a little. Back in October, when Mama and Daddy had come to the school to stand up for her, she had liked them being her guardian angels. But this was way different, she decided—and way confusing.

She ran her hand over the top of her very-short-but-shiny light brown hair like she always did when she was confused, and she closed her eyes. Time to imagine Jesus. And of course, there he was, with his kind eyes, waiting for her questions.

Okay, so what is WITH Mama and Daddy lately? she murmured to him in her mind. *The baby that hasn't even been born yet has more privacy than I do!*

Sophie opened her eyes and squirmed some more. It didn't feel exactly right to be complaining to Jesus about her parents. There was that whole "honor your father and mother" thing to consider.

She was still pondering it when she got to her locker. Most of the other Corn Flakes were waiting for her. That was the name they'd given themselves when the Corn Pops, the wickedly popular girls, had said they were "flakes." To the Corn Flakes, that meant they were free to be themselves and never put down other people the way the Corn Pops did.

"How come you weren't online last night?" Fiona tucked back the wayward strand of golden-brown hair that was always creeping over one magic-gray eye. "I wanted to IM you. I tried emailing, but you didn't answer."

"Guess," Sophie said. She dropped her backpack and went after her combination lock.

"Lacie had another paper to write," said Darbie O'Grady. She swept both sides of her reddish bob behind her ears. "I bet you were up to ninety."

In Darbie's Irish slang, that meant Sophie was ready to explode. Sophie nodded and yanked her locker open.

"You're so lucky you're an only child, Darbie," she said. "You too, Mags."

"Huh." The sound that came out of Maggie LaQuita was as square and solid as everything else about her, including the blunt cut of her Cuban-dark hair.

"You don't have other siblings reading your emails and getting into your stuff," Fiona said. "Not like Sophie and I do."

"But my mother is the only other person in my house," Maggie said. "If I close the door to my room, she says I'm shutting her out."

Sophie looked up, her literature book poised in midair. "Really?" she said. "I thought you and your mom got along really good. She makes all your clothes and everything."

"Huh," Maggie said again. She looked down at the bright turquoise-and-orange poncho that covered her chest. "She hasn't figured out that we don't have the same tastes anymore."

"And does she say you're giving her cheek when you complain?" Darbie said.

Maggie frowned. "You mean like I'm talking back to her?"

"Yeah."

Maggie's dark eyes answered for her.

"I have the same problem," Darbie said. She leaned against the bank of lockers opposite Sophie's. "When I first came here, I liked it that Aunt Emily and Uncle Patrick were always protecting me from scary things. But I've adjusted — "

"You're practically American now," Fiona added.

"But they still turn the channel every time someone says a cross word on the telly, and they look at me like I might go mental."

Sophie gave her locker door another shove and smiled at all of them.

"What?" Fiona said.

"I'm glad we all have parent problems," she said. "I mean, I'm not glad about the problems, but I'm glad at least we all understand what we're going through."

"So we can empathize," Fiona said.

"Define," Maggie said.

"It's better than sympathizing, where you just think you know how somebody feels. When you empathize, you really *do* know how the other person feels."

"That's why we're the Corn Flakes, isn't it?" Darbie said.

"Is empathizing part of the Corn Flake Code?" Maggie said.

Fiona counted off on her fingers. "Never put anybody down even though they do it to you. Don't fight back or give in to bullies; just take back your power to be yourself. Talk to Jesus about everything because he gives you the power to be who he made you to be."

"I didn't hear anything about empathizing," Maggie said, words thudding.

"It's got to be in there somewhere," Darbie said.

"We can add it," Sophie said. "Corn Flakes are totally loyal to each other and will always empathize."

"I love it," Fiona said. "And a Corn Flake will help you with the things your parents can't help you with." Her pink bow of a mouth went into a grin. "Like dealing with *them*!"

"Who are we dealing with?" another voice chimed in.

Sophie shoved her shoulder against her locker door, which still wouldn't close, as Willoughby Wiley joined them. Her wildly curly brown hair was springing out of a messy bun in just the right way, and her hazel eyes were shining. Sophie always thought you didn't have to see the red, white, and blue Great Marsh Middle School pom-poms sticking out of her backpack to know she was a cheerleader.

"We were talking about parents," Fiona said.

"And I'm talking about you getting away from my locker so I can get in it—please."

That came from Julia Cummings, the tall, auburn-haired leader of the Corn Pops, who had trailed in behind Willoughby with her fellow Pops at her heels. On-the-chubby-side B.J. Schneider nearly plowed into the back of Julia as she glared at Willoughby.

Cheerleader envy, Sophie thought. The Corn Pops were still mad that they had been kicked off the seventh-grade cheerleading squad while Willoughby, a former Corn Pop herself, was now captain. *But they don't dare do anything about it or they're toast*, Sophie added to herself. They'd gotten into enough trouble for harassing the Flakes to last them until graduation.

Which was probably why, Sophie decided, Julia gave Darbie an icy smile as Darbie said, "Oh, sorry," and stepped away from Julia's locker. Pale, thin Corn Pop Anne-Stuart sniffed at Darbie as she moved, but, then, Anne-Stuart was always sniffing. Sophie had never known her not to be in dire need of a box of tissues.

"You're not supposed to touch other people's lockers," Cassie said to Darbie. She tossed her very long, almost-too-blonde hair as if she were adding punctuation. Cassie was the newest of the Corn Pops. It seemed to Sophie that she was always trying to prove herself, especially to Julia.

Willoughby turned her back on them completely and widened her eyes at the Flakes. "What about parents?" she said. "You all looked bummed."

Darbie groaned and Maggie filled her in, with Fiona adding details. Sophie listened while she fought with her locker door, which was now jammed half open and half closed.

"You know what?" Willoughby said. "Maybe it's because I just have a dad and not a mom, but I have way a lot of freedom. Ya'll can escape to my house anytime."

The bell rang. "How about now?" Fiona said. "I don't really want to go see that lame gang movie." She gave Sophie a sympathetic — or maybe empathetic — look.

"You better come on," Maggie said to Sophie as they all hurried toward the hall.

"You all go ahead," Sophie said. "I have to get this thing open so I can close it."

"That makes total sense," Julia muttered as she and the Corn Pops sailed away.

"Makes sense to us," Fiona said. Although there wasn't time for the official Corn Flake pinky promise shake, she held up her little finger and wiggled it, and the rest of the girls did the same.

I would LOVE to escape to Willoughby's, like, tonight! Sophie thought as she put one foot up on the locker below hers to brace herself for one more tug. But then she felt a guilt pang. *I want to escape from my own house?*

She pulled on the locker with both hands, but her fingers slipped off and she dropped to her seat on the floor. At the end

of the row of lockers, feet rushed past, and she was sure she heard Colton Messik say, "Oops, Soapy, you fell. Too bad."

He was one of the absurd little creep boys the Corn Flakes had named the Fruit Loops. At least there were only two of them now, since Eddie Wornom was no longer around.

Two too many, Sophie thought as she got to her feet and readjusted her glasses. *I need to escape from them too.*

Actually, she thought, as she gave up on getting the locker open and shoved at it with her backpack to get it closed, she didn't really need to go to Willoughby's or anywhere else to shut it all out. Escape was never more than a dream character away.

And do I need one now or what? Sophie thought. *Hello!*

She stopped pushing and headed for the hall. Somebody who could protect the right of kids to grow up — that's what she saw taking shape in her dream-mind. Maybe the leader of a good gang.

What could her name be? Goodie?

Nah, too sappy.

My name will be revealed on a need-to-know basis, thought the tough little woman with the smooth muscles that made her T-shirt sleeves curve outward. I don't tell it to just any punk who shoves me in a crowd, she told herself as she dodged passing elbows like a championship boxer. They can see that I can't be pushed around.

But though she was tough, she didn't swagger. It was sheer confidence that drove her straight into the thick of the danger on the street —

"Sophie LaCroix — do you want to tell me what you're doing down here?"

Sophie blinked and found herself standing in the middle of an eighth-grade hall.

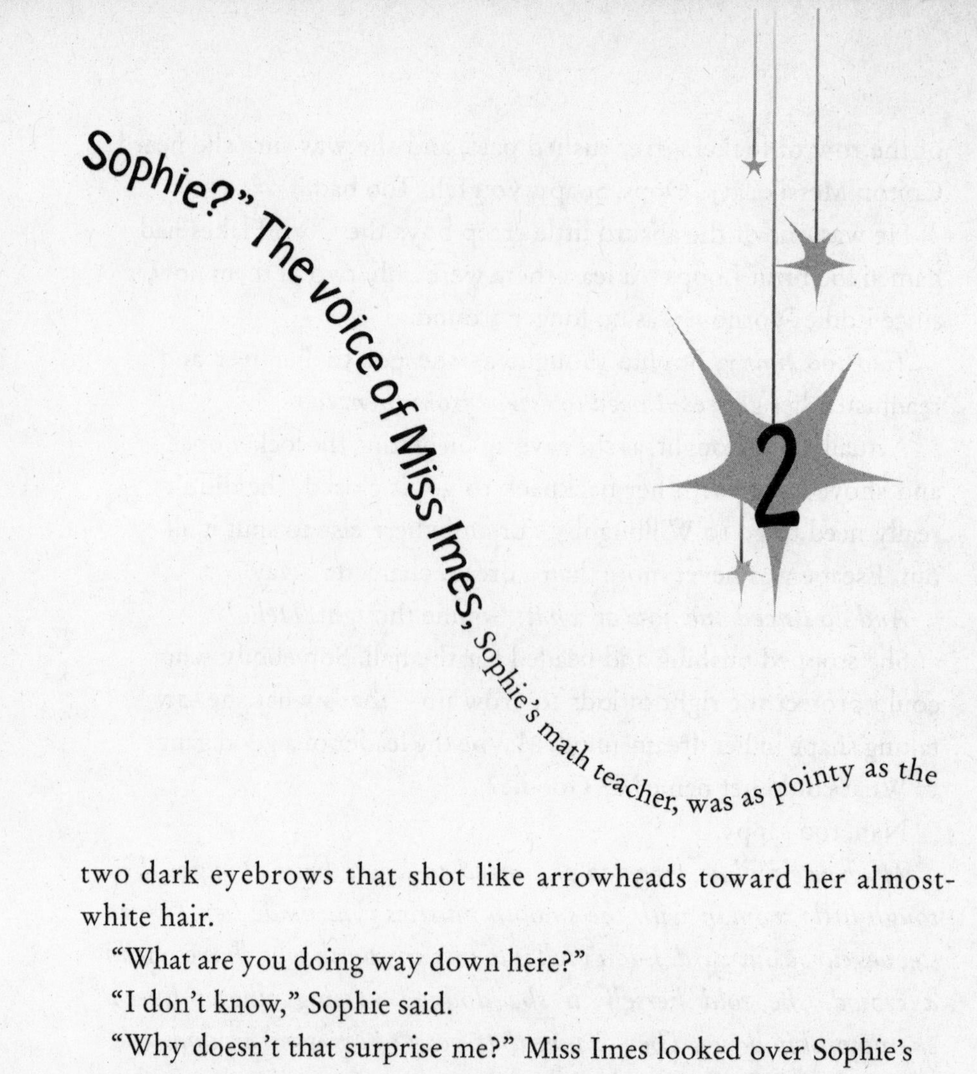

2

Sophie?" The voice of Miss Imes, Sophie's math teacher, was as pointy as the two dark eyebrows that shot like arrowheads toward her almost-white hair.

"What are you doing way down here?"

"I don't know," Sophie said.

"Why doesn't that surprise me?" Miss Imes looked over Sophie's head at the students surging past. "Slow it down. You'll all get a seat."

Nobody talked back. *Even eighth graders don't mess with her*, Sophie thought. Rumor had it that eighth graders really didn't take orders from anybody. She'd never had a chance to check that out firsthand. She'd never even been in an eighth-grade hall.

"You'd best get yourself to class before you're marked tardy," Miss Imes said to her. "I don't want you getting into any trouble that will keep you out of the new Film Club project."

"What new project?" Sophie could feel her eyes popping.

"You'll find out at lunch," Miss Imes said. "It's exciting."

Nothing actually sounded exciting when it came dryly out of Miss Imes' mouth. After all, she was a math teacher. But if she said it was, it was.

"No tardies," Miss Imes said.

Sophie turned and followed the throng toward the main hall where she could cross to seventh-grade territory.

And the sooner the better, she thought.

It was different down here. There were boy-girl couples holding hands and girls striding as if they were going down a fashion show runway and guys spewing out language Sophie hadn't heard since Eddie Wornom had been sent away to military school.

But even all that didn't dampen the promise of a new project. Sophie went into a higher gear. No way was she going to be late and mess up being able to participate.

Not only that, she thought as she ducked around a hugging couple, *I don't want to get kicked off Round Table either.*

Round Table was the handpicked council of students and faculty members who figured out how to help kids who got in trouble and needed to change more than they needed punishment.

The tough little good-gang leader quickened her steps. There was so much work to be done. The more punk-wannabes she could get out of trouble, the better.

Sophie was three long leaps from her first-period-classroom door when the final bell rang. She slipped in just as it was closing — one of the few benefits of being the smallest kid in the seventh grade.

Inside, everybody was standing up, yelling, "Here!" as Ms. Hess, the younger of the two English/history block teachers, called out their names so they could head to the gym for the movie.

Fiona grabbed Sophie's arm. "I answered for you. There's so much confusion in here Ms. Hess didn't even notice."

"I'm glad it wasn't Mrs. Clayton," Sophie said. Not only was the other teacher older and sharper, she was the head of the Round Table.

"Wish you were coming with," Darbie said as Ms. Hess herded the class out.

Sophie nodded miserably and stepped aside so Julia and Anne-Stuart could pass.

"What are you hanging back for?" Anne-Stuart said through her nose.

"Not going," Sophie said.

Anne-Stuart exchanged glances with Julia, and they both curled their lips.

"Oh," Julia said. "I get it."

No, you do not "get it," Sophie thought as they gave her a final smirk and exited. She was pretty sure they didn't know what *empathize* meant. She was grateful for the pinky fingers Darbie and Fiona wiggled at her as they left.

But Sophie still felt like a loser as she went up to Mrs. Clayton's desk. "My dad wouldn't sign my permission slip," she said to the top of Mrs. Clayton's cement-like helmet of yellowy-blonde hair. "He thinks it's too violent."

Mrs. Clayton bulleted a long look at her before she said in her trumpet voice, "I'll write you a library pass for first and second periods." At least she added, "I can trust you."

That didn't make Sophie feel any less out of it. But when she walked into the library, she could feel a smile spreading from ear to ear.

"Kitty!" she said.

"Shhh!" the librarian said.

Sophie hurried over to the set of shelves where her friend Kitty Munford, the final Corn Flake, was flipping listlessly through a book. Her face, pale and puffy, seemed to fill with light when she saw Sophie.

It was hard to hug somebody who was sitting in a wheelchair, but Sophie managed. She'd just seen Kitty on Sunday, but now that Kitty was being homeschooled while she was having chemotherapy for her leukemia, Sophie missed being with her every day.

"What are you doing here?" Sophie whispered as she squatted beside the chair Kitty used when she got too weak to walk.

"My mom's talking to somebody in the office," Kitty said. "I'm supposed to be checking out some books, but I'm sick of reading."

Sophie nodded. She hoped she looked empathetic, since she had never been as sick as Kitty was and had no idea what it must be like. From the tired look in Kitty's blue eyes and the lack of hair under her pink-and-black-tweed hat, Sophie knew it must be pretty awful. The hair was the only thing she *could* empathize with, since she'd shaved her head at the beginning of the year so Kitty wouldn't have to be bald alone. Sophie's was growing back in. Kitty's wasn't.

Kitty folded her fingers weakly around Sophie's arm. "Are you doing another Corn Flakes production soon?"

"Yes!" Sophie said. "Miss Imes says it's going to be something special."

"Can I please, *please* be in it? I'm going nutso being at home."

"Of course you can!" Sophie said. "You're a Corn Flake."

"My mom is driving me bonkers, Sophie. She 'protects' me every single minute!"

Sophie nodded. She was sure she was empathizing now. "I hear you. We *all* hear you. Just about everybody's parents are, like, smothering them."

Kitty tugged at her hat. "Mom's totally in my space all the time."

"Don't worry," Sophie said. "We'll make a part in the film for you."

"You're saving my life," Kitty said.

When Kitty's mother bustled into the library looking like she expected to find Kitty passed out on the floor, Sophie was sure Kitty hadn't been exaggerating.

"Mom, Sophie says I can be in the next movie!" Kitty said.

"Shhh!" the librarian said.

"We'll see," Mrs. Munford said.

When she'd pushed Kitty out the door, with Kitty grabbing at the wheels of her chair and saying, "Mom — I can do it!" Sophie found a corner and began to see ...

The good-gang leader still did not expose her name to the world. But she did reveal what she was about. With her gang of good-hearted members gathered around her, hanging on every tough-love word that came from her lips, she explained to them how they needed to protect the right of every kid on the streets to grow up to be independent and unafraid. "It's a jungle out there," she told them, eyes intense beneath the bill of her ball cap. "Everyone is telling them who to be, but we can't let them get tangled up — "

By the time the bell rang for third period, Good-Something was fully formed. Sophie dashed to PE ready to reveal her to the Flakes in the locker room.

Marching forward on her short but muscular legs, she could feel the desperate kids following her. They were waiting for their street orders, and she was ready to deliver them, just as soon as she got through this crowd of unruly boys who obviously didn't need protection and support as much as they needed somebody to teach them some manners. They were spilling out from a clogged doorway, blocking her path, but Good-Something lowered her head and plowed right through them. Oh, but her spirit was mightier than her body, and she felt herself going down — until a large hand seemed to come down from the heavens and lift her up —

"Little Bit, you want to get yourself trampled?"

Sophie felt her feet hit solid ground again as Coach Nanini, the boys' PE teacher, set her down in the hallway, apart from the mob of boys pushing into the locker room.

"I must have lost my head," Sophie said. She grinned at him. He grinned back, his one big eyebrow crumpling down over his eyes. He always reminded her of a big happy gorilla with no hair. To her, he was Coach Virile.

"You're going to lose worse than your head if you get under those animals' feet," he said. He handed Sophie her glasses, which he'd obviously rescued.

"I'll lose *worse* if I don't get to roll call on time," Sophie said as she put them back on.

"You got that right." Coach Virile leaned down and lowered his high-pitched-for-a-huge-guy voice. "I wouldn't cross Coach Yates today. She's a little grumpy."

More than usual? Sophie wanted to say. The girls' PE teacher yelled more than Sophie's father did when he was watching the Dallas Cowboys on TV. Sophie hurried into the locker room. Fiona, Darbie, and Maggie were already there changing.

"You are so lucky you missed that movie, Soph," Fiona said instead of hello.

Darbie nodded through the neck hole of her T-shirt as she poked her head in. "I nearly went mental with boredom."

"Our films are a lot better," Maggie said.

Sophie knew they were all lying, but she appreciated it. Besides, they'd reminded her of what Miss Imes had said about a new Film Club project. She was explaining when Willoughby dashed in, backpack flying out behind her.

"You're gonna be late for roll call," Maggie said, voice matter-of-fact.

"I know!" Willoughby said. She tried to slide her backpack off, but the strap caught on her sweater.

"Stop before you hurt yourself," Fiona said. "Come on, guys."

The Corn Flakes went into action, Maggie and Darbie stripping off Willoughby's backpack, sweater, tank top, and jeans, while Sophie and Fiona pulled on her sweatshirt and track pants as soon as there was a place to put them.

"Give me your arm," Sophie said, holding out the sleeve of the sweatshirt.

But Fiona had Willoughby focused on shoving her foot into a tennis shoe, so Sophie took the arm herself.

Willoughby yelped. She was always shrieking in a voice that reminded Sophie of a poodle, but this was different. Willoughby pulled back her arm and cradled it.

"Did I grab you too hard?" Sophie said.

"No," Willoughby said. "I hurt it last night. I was practicing a new cheer and I fell over the coffee table." She did give her poodle-laugh then. "I'm such a klutz."

"You guys carry her while I get this other shoe on her," Fiona said.

They made it to the line in time for roll call, but not without a stony stare from Coach Yates. Her graying ponytail seemed to pinch her face even tighter than usual, and Sophie decided Coach Virile had been right.

By the time she got through PE and Miss Imes' fourth-period math class, Sophie was sure she would unzip and come right out of her skin if she didn't find out what the special film project was. All the Film Club members met in Miss Imes' classroom at lunch. That included the Corn Flakes and the boys they thought of as the Lucky Charms – because they never acted heinous the way the Fruit

Loops did and were actually fun sometimes. When Mr. Stires, their other adviser and also their science teacher, arrived, Miss Imes, as Willoughby put it, dished.

"There is going to be a film festival in one month," she said. "Schools from three counties have been invited to participate. Each entry is to follow the theme 'Bringing History to Life Today.'"

Sophie squealed. Could that have been any more perfect? The Corn Flakes had been making movies about history for a whole year. And Jimmy, Nathan, and Vincent were such huge history buffs, they had their own swords and swashbuckler boots.

Even now, Vincent, who was skinny and had a big, loose grin that filled up most of his face, was waving his arm.

"Did you want to say something, Vincent?" Mr. Stires said with the usual chuckle. He thought just about everything students did was amusing. Even his toothbrush mustache always looked cheerful.

"Seeing that movie this morning made me think of this," Vincent said. His voice cracked, which it did a lot. Whenever Vincent's voice cracked, Nathan's face turned red. But, then, Nathan's face was always turning red.

"No offense, Vincent," Fiona said, "but I don't think gangs are history."

Vincent wiggled his eyebrows. "Nineteen-twenties gangs are."

There was a thinking-silence.

"You mean, like gangsters and Al Capone and tommy guns?" Jimmy said. He was quieter than the other two Charms, but when he said something, everybody listened. The Corn Pops, Sophie had noticed, listened because Jimmy was also blond and tanned and had muscles from being in gymnastics.

"I know about the twenties," Darbie said. "They did the Charleston and swallowed goldfish back then."

"I'm not doing that," Maggie said.

"We could have some really good characters," Vincent said. "Guys with names like Bugsy— "

"Goodsy!" Sophie said.

Nathan cocked his curly head, topped as always with a Redskins ball cap. "I don't remember a gangster named Goodsy." He reddened.

"I think she's talking about a new character," Fiona said. She leaned into Sophie. "What have you got, Soph?"

Sophie launched into Goodsy—Goodsy Malone—and the rest of the group listened. Vincent added ideas, and his voice cracked more with each one, which meant he was excited. Jimmy nodded. Maggie pulled out the Corn Flakes Treasure Book to take notes. Nathan turned a happier red, and Willoughby was already designing twenties hairdos on binder paper.

"I think it's our best idea yet," Fiona said.

"A lot of people are going to see this," Miss Imes said, "so you want it to be the best you can do."

"It will be," Sophie promised her.

"Let's all take a vow to give it 200 percent," Fiona said.

"I think it only goes up to 100," Vincent said.

"I'm in," Jimmy said. Everybody else agreed. Then they all looked at Sophie. She was always the director.

"Okay," she said. "We start doing research today after school. Meet in the library— "

"I can't," Willoughby said. "I have cheerleading practice."

"That's not 100 percent," Maggie said.

But Sophie put her hand up. "We already knew Willoughby has practice every school day. You can meet other times, right?"

Willoughby nodded until her curls bounced like springs.

"Let's cut her some slack," Sophie said. She was sure that was something the tough but bighearted—and definitely empathetic—Goodsy Malone would say.

3

Right after sixth period, Sophie ran for the pay phone near the gym to call Mama before the after-school line formed. Her mother's voice was thin when she answered.

"I need to stay after, okay?" Sophie said. "We have a new Film Club project — we're going to be in a *festival* — wait 'til I tell you about it — "

"Soph — "

"I can take the late bus — "

"Sophie." Mama's voice stretched like a rubber band. "You have to watch Zeke, remember?"

Sophie didn't mean for the impatient, "Aw, man," to slip out, but it did.

"I'm sorry," Mama said, "but I'm feeling really puny. I'm afraid Zeke will try to Spider-Man his way up the side of the house if nobody's watching him."

Mama tried to laugh. Sophie didn't.

"Things are going to be a lot easier after this little one is born, Dream Girl," Mama said.

But even Mama's pet name for her — the one that always showed she really did understand who Sophie was — added a link to the imaginary chain around her ankle.

"Z-Boy won't be home for half an hour," Mama said. "That gives you a little time with your friends."

If the bus wasn't leaving, like, right this minute, Sophie wanted to say. As it was, there was barely time to sprint to the library to deliver the bad news to the club and race to the front of the school. When she finally got there, panting like a dog, the bus was already leaving.

"No!" she called after it. Her voice squeaked up.

"Miss your bus?" said an all-too-familiar voice. The expected sniff followed.

"What'll you do now?" B.J. chimed in.

"I'd call a cab," Julia said. "But that's just me."

Cassie gave her stringy tresses a toss. "Use your cell phone. Oh, wait — you don't have one!"

Only the Corn Flake Code kept Sophie from rolling her eyes at all of them. She turned away and Willoughby popped up, curls dancing in the wind.

"I have a cell phone, Soph," she said. "You want to call your mom?"

"Since when did *you* get a cell phone, Willoughby?" B.J. said.

Julia snapped the Pops away with her fingers. Willoughby produced a pink phone from the pocket of her track pants, flipped it open, and pulled up the antenna with her teeth.

"Where did you get this?" Sophie said.

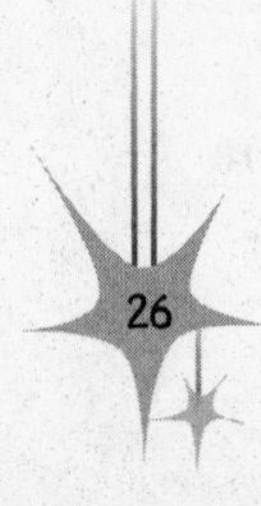

"My dad. He spoils me." Willoughby poised a finger over the tiny buttons. "I already have your number programmed in."

"Can we call the high school instead?" Sophie said. "I need to find Lacie."

It took a while to leave a message, then wait for Lacie to call back. Willoughby stood first on one foot and then the other and glanced at her watch every seven seconds. Sophie was afraid she'd have to give her back the phone and let her go where she was obviously dying to get to. But it burst into a tinny version of "It's a Small World," and Willoughby shrieked, "Answer it!"

"Whose phone do you have?" Lacie said when Sophie said hello.

"I need you to take my Zeke duty today," Sophie said. "Please? It's vital."

"Yeah, I'm sure it's a matter of life and death." There was a pause. "You are so going to owe me for this."

"Thank you!" Sophie cried. She knew she sounded like Willoughby, who looked like she was about to let out a poodle-yelp herself if she didn't get to wherever. Sophie hung up before Lacie could elaborate on just *how* she was going to owe her.

Whatever it was, it was worth it, Sophie decided when she was deep into research in the library. The 1920s were, in Fiona's words, "positively scintillating."

"Does that mean it gives you chills?" Sophie said.

"Precisely," Fiona said.

Maggie grunted from behind a book called *Fashions of the Jazz Age* where she was getting ideas for her mom to make their costumes. "I don't feel any chills," she said.

But all of it made goose bumps chase across Sophie's skin.

The girls of the twenties, called flappers, bobbed their hair and shortened their skirts to be free of the shackles of Victorian corsets and gowns.

The college boys in oversize fur coats sat on top of flagpoles and swallowed goldfish, just because they could.

The good people of Chicago tried to reclaim their city from the corruption of mob leaders like Al Capone. That was what made Sophie suggest that Goodsy Malone should be a police officer instead of a gang leader.

"They didn't have female cops back then," Vincent said. He squinted at the computer screen. "Women had barely gotten the right to vote."

"So I'll play a boy," Sophie said. She ran a hand over her head. "I've got the hair for it."

Jimmy jabbed a thumb toward the computer. "This says girls made a lot of advances in the twenties. Maybe we could make it like Goodsy is a girl, but she's pretending to be a guy so she can be a cop." He shrugged his big gymnast's shoulders. "It's just an idea."

"It's brilliant," Fiona said.

Goodsy Malone pulled her fedora low over her eyes the way the other plainclothes detectives did and was grateful for her bobbed hair. For once it was even a good thing to be the flattest-chested woman in America. There wasn't a chance anyone would guess her secret, and with Al Capone's mob pumping out bullets with their tommy guns all over town, the Chicago coppers needed all the help they could get—

"You didn't hear any of that, did you, Sophie?" Maggie said. She closed the Treasure Book.

Sophie peeked out from under the bill of her newsboy cap and shook her head.

"Vincent's going to email us with more information tonight," Fiona said. "Then we can finish the outline."

"This is going to be brilliant," Darbie said.

"It's gonna be swell," Nathan said. His face went radish-colored as they all stared at him. "I was looking up slang. They said 'swell' instead of 'cool.'"

"Let's all start saying that," Sophie said.

She said it in her head all the way to the late bus. The word fit Goodsy's lips as if it were made for them.

Taking the bus is a swell way to spy on the mob, Goodsy told herself as she scanned the passing city with trained eyes. They'll never think of it, and they'll let their guard down. Maybe she would see them attempt one of the drive-by shootings. That would be really *swell.*

Even as the thought appeared, so did a long black car with darkly tinted windows. It slowed to a crawl in front of a small grocery store, and Goodsy watched as the glass in the back opened and the barrel of a gun inched its way out. Before Goodsy could shout for the driver to stop the bus, she heard the shots rat-a-tat-tatting in rapid succession.

"Everybody down!" she shouted—and dived under the seat. Around her the crowd roared—

With laughter.

"Hey," one of the eighth-grade boys said. "There's a chick freaking out back here."

Gill's face appeared upside down under Sophie's seat. "What did you think that was?" she said.

"Gunshots," Sophie whispered.

"Dude, it was that eighth grader's cell phone. She has it on vibrate, but you can hear it all over."

"Oh," Sophie said. She crept out from under the seat and turned to the window to avoid the okay-she's-whacko looks being cast her way. "Uh-oh," she said.

"Wasn't that your stop back there?" Gill said.

Harley grunted. So did Sophie.

She got off at the next corner and ran back to Odd Road as if Al Capone himself were chasing her—

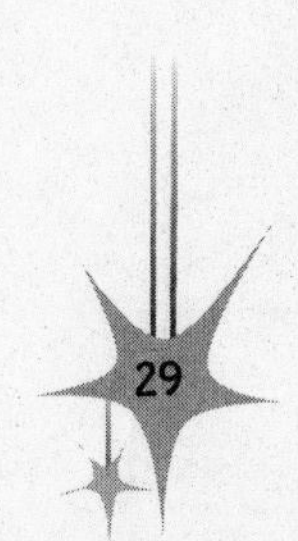

Which he was. Goodsy could hear the soles of his Italian leather shoes slapping the sidewalk as he gained on her, but she hadn't been through vigorous police training for nothing. She veered sharply to the left, leaving the sidewalk as if she were about to dart across the street. The footsteps grew closer as Goodsy ducked between two parked cars.

As soon as she heard the fancy shoes hit grass, she zipped back to the right, leaped over the sidewalk, and ducked behind a pile of leaves. The powerful Al Capone stood bewildered in the middle of the street, head whipping from side to side until he threw up his hands, diamond rings glinting in the sun, and snapped his fingers for the long black car.

Goodsy smiled smugly to herself as the car pulled away with the confused gangster inside. He's never come up against a tough woman before, she thought as she slipped, unnoticed, the rest of the way back to police headquarters. And the beauty of it is, he doesn't even know he has. That was swell.

Goodsy was still feeling pleased with herself when she entered headquarters. That was, until something heavy and warm was suddenly on her back.

"I'm Spider-Man," a six-year-old voice chirped in her ear. "You're goin' down."

"He's all yours," said Lacie, head in the refrigerator. "I'm cooking dinner and Mom's asleep." She pulled her dark head out and waved a bag of shredded cheese in Sophie's direction. "Like I said, you owe me."

"That ain't no problem for me," Sophie said.

Lacie blinked her Daddy-like eyes at Sophie. "It 'ain't'?"

"Matter of fact, it'll be swell." Sophie looked at her brother. "Come on, Z-Boy. I need your help. You're very good with shadows."

Zeke shook his head of unruly dark hair that was looking more like Daddy's every day. "I'm Spider-Man," he said.

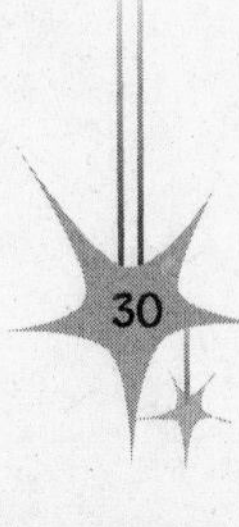

"Swell. Good code name, fella. Capone will never guess it."

Lacie turned back to the counter, ponytail swinging. "I don't even want to know," she said.

Dinner was, as Fiona would have said, nontraditional. They had nachos, the only thing Lacie knew how to make, with celery sticks and peanut butter on the side because Mama had given Lacie instructions to be sure they had a vegetable and some protein. Sophie was sure if Daddy had been there, he would have ordered Anna's Pizza. But he was working late, and it was just the three of them at the snack bar. Sophie got Zeke to eat by promising they'd continue to play "Spider-Man and Goodsy Malone Clean Up Chicago" when he was through.

It was a promise she regretted an hour later when Daddy still wasn't home and Lacie was locked in her room with her algebra book. Every time Sophie pounded on the door for Zeke relief, Lacie just said, "You owe me."

As Sophie tried to do her own math homework, so she wouldn't fall below a B and lose video camera privileges, Zeke climbed up her closet door. Sophie was sure she had paid Lacie back at least twelve times. When Lacie came to the door and said the phone was for Sophie, Sophie tried to pawn Zeke off on her. Then she could at least have a conversation that didn't include peeling him off the shower curtain rod. But Lacie just said, "My meter is still running," and went back to her room.

"Can you hold, please?" Sophie said into the phone. She tucked it under her arm and told Zeke that Al Capone had her locked in the closet. Then she shut the door and barricaded herself behind the clothes.

"I have two minutes, tops," she whispered into the phone.

"That's all I need." The voice on the other end cracked.

"Vincent?" Sophie said.

"I just emailed you a bunch more stuff about Capone," he said. "We have to take him down in our movie. He and his organization

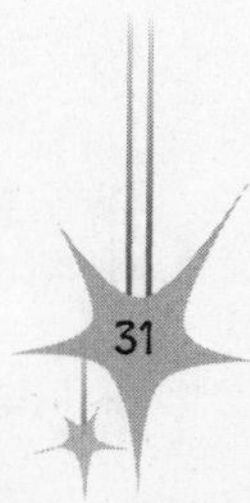

killed all these people and made, like, six million dollars selling illegal alcohol, and the cops couldn't nab him for any of it."

Sophie could feel Goodsy flexing her muscles.

"I'm thinking Jimmy should play him," Vincent said. "He's got the body to be tough, but we'll have to work on the attitude."

Sophie giggled. She had a life-size picture in her mind of Jimmy glowering and chewing on a cigar. The giggles faded as she heard something scraping all the way down the door.

"I'll save you, Goodsy!" a voice chirped. "Even if I have to cut through — "

"No, don't!" Sophie cried.

"Don't what?" Vincent said.

"Nothing." Sophie shoved the door open just in time to snatch a pair of kindergarten scissors out of Zeke's hand. "I'll check my email," she said into the phone.

Yeah, good luck with that, Sophie thought as she hurried downstairs to Daddy's study with Spider-Man crawling down the banister behind her. *I bet Daddy is hiding out at work on purpose.* She gave a Harley-style grunt. *I wish I had a place to hide.*

At least Lacie wasn't on the computer. Sophie gave Zeke a black marker and told him to write a warning letter to Al Capone. Since he was only in first grade and couldn't actually spell anything, she figured that could take a while.

There were emails from Darbie, Fiona, and Willoughby, but Sophie checked Brainchild first. That was Vincent's screen name.

He hadn't been kidding when he said he had more information on Al Capone. There were two pages of facts before Vincent even got to his ideas for scenes.

There was one scene where Capone shot somebody going to worship and left bullet holes in the church wall.

Then he suggested another scene where Goodsy got into the Lexington Hotel and heard Capone planning his next move on

the O'Banyon gang. "We'll have to rig up a chair with a bulletproof back," Vincent had written.

The scene that captured Sophie the most was the one where Capone held Goodsy at gunpoint, and she never even swallowed hard. Sophie could see that one in her mind.

"Gun," Zeke said.

Sophie jumped. She hadn't noticed him scooting onto the chair beside her. He pointed at the screen with a chubby finger, black with marker ink.

"I thought you were writing a letter," Sophie said.

"I'm done." Zeke held up a piece of paper, filled with BAD, EVUL, and even a sentence: SPIDERMAN WIL GET YUO.

"I didn't even know you could spell!" Sophie said.

"Hello," Zeke said. One eyebrow shot up into a where-have-YOU-been position. He poked at Vincent's message on the screen again. "'He will shoot you but o-on-only in the leg.'"

"That's not in the first-grade reader, I can tell you that."

Sophie whipped her head around to see Daddy in the doorway. Zeke bolted for him and clung to his pants.

"Have you had a bath?" Daddy said to him.

"Aw, man, I don't wanna take a bath."

"Then I guess you won't be needing this." Daddy pulled a small Spider-Man action figure out from behind his back. Zeke clattered up the stairs with it before Sophie could even sign off the Internet.

"A little light reading for your baby brother, Soph?" Daddy said. He kissed Sophie on top of the head.

"It's just for our new film project," Sophie said. "It's about the twenties mobsters, and we're taking it to a festival. It's gonna be swell— "

"It's going to be violent from the sounds of it."

As Daddy pulled off his NASA jacket, Sophie stifled a groan, which Daddy also didn't like. *Here we go again*, she thought. Her eyes ached to roll right up into her head.

4

Daddy folded his arms across his big chest. That was never a good sign.

"What is it with you kids and your fascination with violence?" he said.

"The movie's about fighting *against* violence," Sophie said. "It's going to be scintillating."

Daddy's mouth twitched. "I smell Fiona in this."

"It's our whole Film Club. We're doing it for this really cool — really *swell* — festival — "

Daddy put up his hand. "Seriously, Soph, I'm concerned. I don't want all this stuff about guns and gangs in your head."

"It's only a movie, Daddy," Sophie said.

"It's never 'only a movie' with you, Sophie. The next thing I know you'll be staging gun battles in the upstairs hall with Zeke."

"We already did that," Sophie said. Then she wanted to bite her tongue off. *Why do I always have to be so honest?* she thought.

Daddy ran a hand down the back of his head. That was never a good sign either. "I'm going to have a talk with Miss Imes and Mr. Stires before this goes any further," he said.

Sophie felt her mouth drop open, but she couldn't even squeak out a protest.

"I'm not trying to shut down your film," Daddy went on. "I just want to call a time-out so I can see what direction it's taking."

He put his hand on her shoulder. As far as Sophie was concerned, it was part of that shackle around her ankle.

When she climbed into bed later, Sophie dragged the imaginary chain with her. Jesus was there in her mind before she even closed her eyes.

This is heinous! her thoughts cried out to him. *You heard that, I know—Daddy's going to talk to my teachers. Like I'm some first grader! Zeke gets an action figure, and I get a ball and chain.*

Sophie let her eyes fly open. Just like last time, she wasn't sure this was right, complaining to Jesus about her parents.

Dr. Peter says I can tell Jesus anything, she thought. And then she sighed into a purple pillow. She was going to see Dr. Peter the next day at Bible study. Not only was he the most amazing teacher in the entire galaxy, but he had been special to her ever since he'd been her therapist last year. He would know how she should handle this. He always did.

It was hard telling the rest of the Film Club the next morning before school what Daddy planned to do, since they were all so excited about Vincent's ideas.

But Darbie said, "We won't let him make a bags of our project, Sophie," pronouncing it Soophie like she always did. "We're all going to help each other with these eejit parents, remember?"

"And how!"

They all looked at Nathan, who was already going strawberry-colored.

"That means 'you got that right,'" he said. He held up a bunch of papers. "I got a whole list of twenties slang off the Internet."

Sophie grinned. "That's swell, Nathan."

"And how!" Fiona said.

Using phrases like "Says you!" for "You're totally wrong" and "Bushwa!" for "That's a bunch of bunk" almost made Sophie forget about Daddy. Her favorites on the list were the expressions for things that were even better than swell. Like "That's the bee's knees!" or "the cat's pajamas!" The girls were speaking twenties slang like a second language by the time they got to third-period PE.

In the locker room, they filled Willoughby in as much as they could before Coach Yates started bellowing — louder than usual — for them to hurry up.

"Okay, here's the deal," Fiona said as they all headed for roll call. "We need more time with you, Will, to get you caught up, so let's do a sleepover at my house Friday night."

"And we'll see if Kitty can come," Sophie said. "It'll be swell."

"I can't make it."

They all looked at Willoughby, who was twirling a curl around her finger.

"Says you!" Fiona said.

"I have a cheerleading thing."

"Practice is only after school," Maggie said, words coming out in fact blocks.

"It isn't exactly practice," Willoughby said. She was still twirling the curl, so tightly that the end of her finger was turning purple. "Well, it's kind of like practice, only not like regular practice — it's sort of practice for practice."

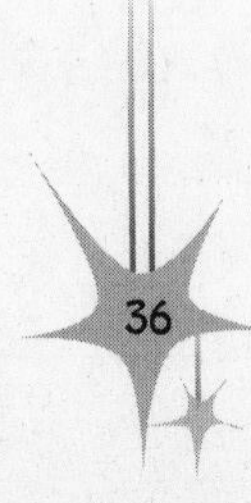

Fiona blinked. "That made absolutely no sense at all."

Sophie wasn't sure it did to Willoughby either. Willoughby's forehead was pulled into folds, and she seemed relieved when Coach Yates yelled for them all to line up for basketball drills.

That was only one of the things on Sophie's mind when they got to Bible study class that afternoon. In spite of the fun they were having with "the cat's pajamas," she hadn't forgotten completely about Daddy pushing himself right into the middle of her business.

That was the good — *swell* — thing about Dr. Peter. He could make Bible study about any problem the girls — Fiona, Sophie, Maggie, Darbie, Gill, and Harley — brought in. There was nothing they'd faced yet in middle school that Dr. Peter couldn't find in the Bible somewhere. Sophie was convinced he had the whole thing memorized.

The second-best thing about Dr. Peter's Bible study was the fact that he had different-colored beanbag chairs with matching Bible covers, and there was always some kind of "sumptuous snack treat," as Fiona put it. Today it was sub sandwiches on big hunky wheat rolls cut into girl-size slices.

But the best was Dr. Peter himself. He was a much smaller man than Sophie's father, but he seemed to fill up a room with his sparkle. Blue eyes twinkled behind his glasses, and there was always a smile on his face and a zany gel-gleam to his short, curly hair.

As they selected their mini-sandwiches from the tray, he rubbed his hands together the way he always did when he was excited to get started.

"Whatcha got for me today?" he said.

Each one of them got a turn, between bites, to talk about the stuff they'd had to deal with since last Wednesday. Everybody, including Harley and Gill, complained about parents and brothers and sisters and the total lack of privacy in the seventh-grade world.

When they were all finished whining, and half the sandwiches had been wolfed down, Dr. Peter worked his glasses up by wrinkling his nose, like he always did.

"I think I have a story for you," he said.

"Swell," Sophie said.

"That's the bee's knees, Dr. P.," Fiona said.

"The cat's pajamas," Darbie put in.

"Let me guess," Dr. Peter said, "you're working on a twenties film." His eyes did their twinkle-thing. "That's the elephant's eyebrows."

Sophie saw Maggie jot that down.

Dr. Peter told them all to settle back in their beanbags and close their eyes. "I'm going to read Matthew 12, verses 1 through 8," he said. "So get ready to imagine."

Sophie never had to do much getting ready. She loved this way of studying the Bible.

"Jesus has been teaching for awhile now," Dr. Peter said. "People are starting to believe what he's telling them, and that doesn't make the Pharisees happy."

I hope we don't have to imagine we're one of them, Sophie thought. The Pharisees were the ones who were always trying to make everybody follow a bunch of strict rules and bad-mouthing Jesus.

"Pretend in your mind that you are one of the disciples," Dr. Peter said.

Sophie grinned to herself. *Now you're talkin'*, she thought. Nathan would be pleased that she was using his list.

"'At that time Jesus went through the grainfields on the Sabbath,'" Dr. Peter read. "'His disciples were hungry and began to pick some heads of grain and eat them.'"

Although Sophie would rather have dreamed up a hot order of fries, she tried to imagine herself plucking the top off a stalk

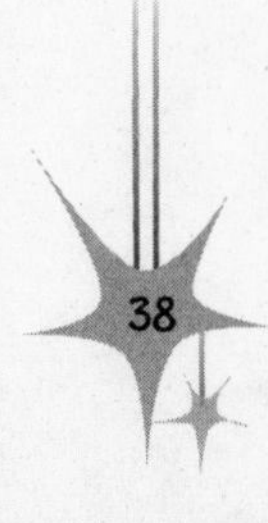

of wheat and munching away as she hurried to get up closer to Jesus. She didn't want to miss a word he said, and her stomach was rumbling so loud she was afraid she would. She couldn't crunch the grain in her mouth fast enough.

"'When the Pharisees saw this, they said to him, "Look! Your disciples are doing what is unlawful on the Sabbath."'"

Sophie/disciple scowled as she chewed. Why were those pinch-faced men always coming around messing things up? She glanced anxiously at Jesus. The only time he really got angry was when he was talking to them, and it wasn't pretty. Besides, the Pharisees always made her feel like she'd done something wrong, even when she hadn't. She inched closer to Jesus and waited for the explosion.

"'He answered, "Haven't you read what David did when he and his companions were hungry? He entered the house of God, and he and his companions ate the consecrated bread — which was not lawful for them to do, but only for the priests."'"

"They ate what kind of bread?" Maggie said.

Sophie sighed. It was hard to stay in Bible-character with facts-only Maggie around.

"Consecrated," Dr. Peter said. "Every Sabbath, like our Sunday, the priests had to set twelve fresh loaves of bread on a table in the Holy Place. That bread was set aside as an offering to God."

"Okay, go on," Maggie said.

Sophie slipped back into disciple mode.

"Wait," Fiona said. Sophie groaned silently. "Why did David do that if it wasn't allowed?"

"He was running away from Saul, who was trying to kill him," Dr. Peter said. "He had no food, he was hungry, and he needed strength for the things he'd have to do. So the priests gave him and his friends the consecrated bread." His eyes twinkled. "Let me read on, and you'll see what this is about."

Sophie's disciple was all but tapping his sandaled toe.

"Jesus goes on to say," Dr. Peter said, "'"Or haven't you read in the Law that on the Sabbath the priests in the temple desecrate the day and yet are innocent?"'"

Yeah, Sophie/disciple wanted to say to the frowning Pharisees, *haven't you read that?*

Come to think of it, had *she* even read that? She stuffed another handful of grain into her mouth and crept even closer to Jesus. She hoped he would explain.

But it was Dr. Peter who was talking now. "Nobody was supposed to do their customary work on the Sabbath," he was saying, "except the priests. They had to perform the special Sabbath sacrifices, which was their work in the temple. So technically they desecrated the day — disobeyed the commandment about the Sabbath — but they were innocent because that was what they were supposed to do." Dr. Peter's voice went back into his Jesus tone. "' "I tell you that one greater than the temple is here. If you had known what these words mean, " 'I desire mercy, not sacrifice,' " you would not have condemned the innocent. For the Son of Man is Lord of the Sabbath." '"

Sophie/disciple wasn't sure what all that meant, but her chest swelled proudly. *You tell 'em, Jesus*, she thought. *Put those Pharisees in their place.*

"I don't get it," Maggie said.

Sophie sighed again and abandoned the disciple. Everyone else's eyes were open too. Dr. Peter's were twinkly again.

"As usual, the Pharisees were all about the rules of the Sabbath," he said. "But they didn't understand what it really meant to keep the Sabbath day holy. If they had been in the temple when David and his men came in there practically starving, they would have said, 'Too bad. Come back tomorrow and we'll feed you.'"

"They could have been dead by then!" Darbie said.

"Exactly!"

Dr. Peter was rubbing his hands together again, as if he had been there. That always made Sophie wish she'd been there too.

"Jesus was saying that it's always lawful to do good and save life, no matter what day it is. The Sabbath was a day about God, and doing good is always about God."

Sophie closed her eyes again, and she could see her kind-eyed Jesus handing out hunks of wheat bread. She could feel a smile wisping across her face.

"Talk to us, Soph," Dr. Peter said.

"I think I get it," Sophie said. "Jesus was like a priest doing his job, only his job was different."

"How so?"

Sophie chewed on that for a second. "He wasn't there to bake loaves of bread for God. He was there to love people and feed them."

"And he was allowed to do that on the Sabbath because he was like a priest," Fiona said.

"Bingo," Dr. Peter said. "And we all can, because we're all priests in a way. We're all ministers for God."

"That's a relief," Maggie said.

Dr. Peter grinned. "Why, Maggie?"

"Because I would get pretty hungry if I couldn't make a sandwich on a Sunday."

"You got any more of those?" Gill said. "This is making *me* hungry."

While Dr. Peter passed the tray around again, Sophie flipped back to the story in her mind.

I don't get what that has to do with us and our parents, she thought. But she still liked the feeling she got whenever Jesus stood up to those razor-faced Pharisees and changed the rules on them.

Sophie wasn't sure if that was what she was supposed to do with Daddy or not. But it sure sounded good.

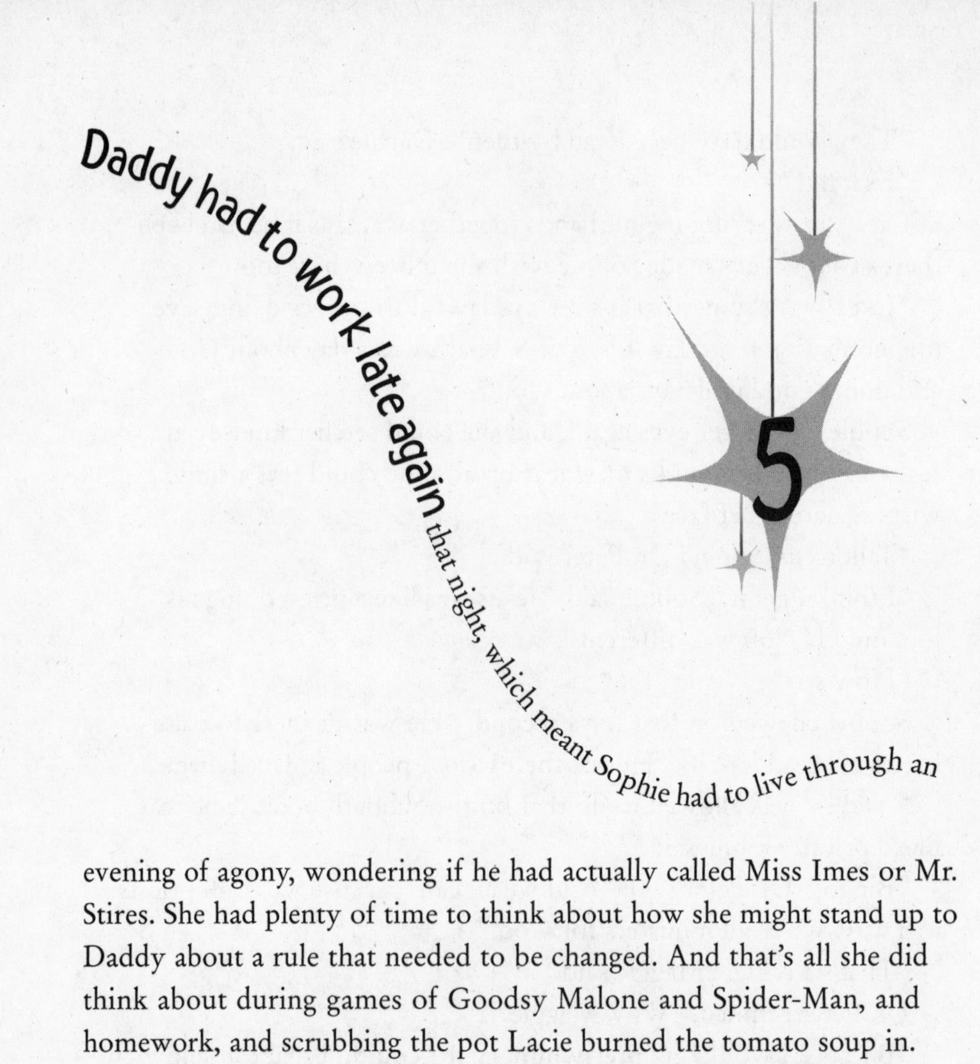

5

Daddy had to work late again that night, which meant Sophie had to live through an evening of agony, wondering if he had actually called Miss Imes or Mr. Stires. She had plenty of time to think about how she might stand up to Daddy about a rule that needed to be changed. And that's all she did think about during games of Goodsy Malone and Spider-Man, and homework, and scrubbing the pot Lacie burned the tomato soup in.

But even she, the daydream queen, had trouble imagining herself toe to toe with Daddy, saying things like, "If you had known what these words mean," and "I tell you one greater than *your* rules is here." The one thing she *could* picture was being grounded for life.

When Zeke was finally in bed, Sophie decided to go back to the Bible story to see if she was missing some magic sentence that would transform her father into a reasonable human being. She was sprawled across her bed, reaching for her Bible, when there was a light tap on the door. Mama poked her curly head in.

"Do you have a minute, Soph?" she said.

Sophie nodded and patted a spot on the bed beside her. Mama made her way across the room, swaying a little from side to side the way Sophie had seen ducks at the park do. Being pregnant made almost everything about Mama different. Her usually elfin face looked more like a chubby cherub's now, and there were soft little puffs of skin under her eyes that Sophie hadn't seen there before. Sophie had only been six when Zeke was born, and she didn't remember a roly-poly mother then.

Mama grabbed a bedpost and hoisted herself up, sinking onto the pink bedspread with a sigh. She sank back into the pile of purple and pink and pale green pillows so that her ponytail of highlighted brown curls tumbled down the side of her face. People always said how much Sophie and Mama looked alike, but Sophie was sure that was definitely not true now.

"I don't know how I'm going to make it all the way to March," Mama said. "It's only November, and I already feel like Humpty Dumpty."

"You want me to make you a cup of hot chocolate or anything?" Sophie said. "I have some Smarties — I'll give you all the green ones."

Mama shook her head, eyes closed. "No. I just want you. Tell me everything about what's going on in your life. I feel like I'm missing it."

Sophie had the sudden urge to curl up beside Mama and rest her head on her belly so she could feel her baby sister swimming around, and to spin out the stories of the last few days so they would last all night. But Mama was still stretching herself into first one position and then another, so Sophie sat cross-legged in front of her.

"Want me to rub your feet?" Sophie said.

"I would love to have you rub my feet," Mama said.

With Mama's puffed-up toes between her kneading hands, Sophie flipped through her memory deck for where to start.

The Film Club — Mama didn't know all about the festival yet.

But Daddy had probably told her about that, and how violent it was, and how he was going to snatch Sophie out of that the way he had with the school movie. Sophie decided not to go there.

The Flakes. Mama always liked to hear what was going on with the girls.

But what was going on with them, besides the film, was all their problems with their parents. Just like hers. Another topic to stay away from.

"I've never seen you at a loss for something to tell me," Mama said. Her eyes looked droopy.

Sophie felt a pang and grabbed for the next thing that came to her mind. "We're a little annoyed with Willoughby right now," she said. That was probably safe.

"Oh?"

"She's way involved in cheerleading, and she's missing a lot of rehearsals for our new film."

"A new film!" Mama said.

Sophie could almost hear the trap she'd landed in snapping shut.

Mama sat up a little straighter against the pillow pile. "So what's it about?"

"Daddy didn't tell you?" Sophie said.

"By the time Daddy gets home I'm already asleep," Mama said. "You probably talk to him more than I do these days."

Unfortunately, Sophie thought.

"Soph?" Mama had her head cocked to the side. "Something wrong between you and Daddy?"

Sophie pretended to concentrate on Mama's instep. This was a place she *definitely* didn't want to go. She didn't even want to drive by.

"Daddy tells me you girls have been such a help," Mama said. "But if you have a problem you need to talk about, don't think we're not here to help *you*." She patted her tummy. "If it's private, your baby sister won't tell."

For an instant, Sophie considered it. Mama was the one who always got her, the one who could make it better with a touch on the cheek or a batch of double-fudge brownies. The one who really could help.

But she'd said "*We're* here to help you." Daddy and Mama hardly ever disagreed when it came to something about the kids, at least not that she and Lacie and Zeke knew about. If Daddy thought telling Miss Imes their film project was too violent was "helping," Mama was sure to go along with it.

And I don't need that kind of help, Sophie thought.

"I'll go get some lotion to rub on your feet," she said.

When she came back from the bathroom, Mama had already drifted off to sleep.

A lot of things have changed with us, Sophie thought as she watched Mama's middle lift and sink with her breathing. It was a sad feeling.

But sad turned to mad the next day at lunch when Sophie and the Flakes arrived in the science room for Film Club. There was Daddy, sitting casually in a student desk, chatting it up with Mr. Stires.

"What in the *world*?" Fiona said, and with good reason.

Boppa, Fiona's balding grandfather, was on the other side of Daddy. Next to him was Darbie's Aunt Emily, nervously clacking her manicured nails. She spoke in low tones to a woman whose face was turning redder with every word. That had to be Nathan's mother.

And the tall man with faded blond hair and arm muscles that showed under his sweater had to be Jimmy's father.

"What is the deal?" Sophie heard Jimmy mutter beside her.

Sophie was sure they all would have stood there, gawking in the doorway, as Darbie put it, if Miss Imes hadn't hurried in behind them and ushered them all to seats. As Fiona sank into the one next to Sophie, she murmured, "Tell your father thanks a lot."

"You tell him," Sophie whispered back. "I don't think I'm speaking to him."

Miss Imes had the parents introduce themselves, and when they got to Aunt Emily, she said she was representing Senora LaQuita, Maggie's mom, too. Willoughby looked at them all sympathetically. It occurred to Sophie that Willoughby and Vincent were the only ones who didn't have an adult there ready to make up their minds for them. Fiona scratched a note to her: *This proves what I've always suspected: Vincent doesn't have parents. He's an adult living in a kid's body.*

Any other time that would have been funny. Right now, nothing was funny.

Miss Imes turned to the kids. "Before you all go completely into shock," she said, "let me explain that I invited your parents here because there has been some question about the content of your new film project."

Guess who asked the question, Sophie thought. So far she hadn't been able to look at her father. She was afraid she would roll her eyes up into her head and never find them again.

"Rather than simply put the kibosh on the entire project," Miss Imes was saying, "I thought it would be more of a learning experience if we all had a voice in setting the limits on the language and violence in the movie. How does that sound to everyone?"

"It sounds like you're going to end up telling us what we can and can't do anyway, so why waste the time?" Fiona said.

Nathan's face turned crimson. So did his mother's. Boppa drew his black, caterpillar eyebrows together the way he always did when Fiona had just embarrassed him to death.

Miss Imes' eyebrows, on the other hand, were stabbing at her hairline. "That is not my intention at all," she said. "In fact, I would like to hear from you students first. Perhaps there is less for your parents to be concerned about than they think. Who would like to start?"

They all looked at Sophie. *I hope I remember to thank them later for putting this whole thing on me*, Sophie thought. This definitely didn't qualify as "the cat's pajamas." Her mind raced, and she was sure she wouldn't squeak out a single thing that made sense—until somebody else stepped in . . .

With her fedora dipped over one eye, Goodsy said, "All right, here's the thing." She hoped her voice was coming out low and rough, because this was no time to have her true identity revealed, not with the entire city council sitting before her. "This is the real world we're living in. We can't pussyfoot around the facts no more, see? There's killing in the streets. There's deals being made behind closed doors that are filling our city with booze and drugs, see? And innocent people are being robbed of their life savings, all in broad daylight. There ain't no way to paint a pretty picture of that. It's real, and we can't deny it, see? It's as plain as the rings on Al Capone's fingers."

"That certainly gives us a sense of the film's flavor," Miss Imes said dryly.

Sophie glanced at Daddy. He had his don't-think-I-don't-know-what-just-happened look on his face.

"I get all that," Aunt Emily said. Her silky Southern accent was a little ruffled. "But how real does it have to be?"

"How real do you think it should be?" Miss Imes said.

Beside Sophie, Fiona stiffened, and Sophie squeezed her wrist so she wouldn't fly out of the seat. But she felt like bursting out with something herself. Something like: *you might as well just let them write the whole thing for us if you're going to do this.*

"No cusswords," Nathan's mother said.

Boppa nodded. "Only as much physical stuff as it takes to suggest violence."

"No actual bloodshed on camera," Daddy put in.

The adults all laughed. Sophie didn't see what was funny.

"I'd like to see more of the problems being solved than see the problems themselves," Jimmy's father said. "Fewer shooting scenes and more discussion of how to fix the situation."

Sophie held on to Fiona with two hands.

There was a long pause. Sophie was sure Miss Imes was deciding which parent to turn the writing of the script over to. But finally Miss Imes nodded at Mr. Stires and said to the kids, "You heard all of that. Can you take that into consideration as you put your film together?"

"That's it?" Fiona said.

"Yes!" Sophie said, squeezing Fiona's wrist until she clamped her mouth shut. "We can definitely do that."

"That'll be swell," Darbie said.

Film Club heads bobbed. Sophie couldn't wait to get out of there and celebrate. *This wouldn't be so bad,* she thought. A surprise victory.

Until Miss Imes said, "All right then. And when the script has been completed, I will email it to each of the parents for approval. I'll contact those who couldn't be here today and let them know." She turned to the students, who all looked to Sophie like birthday balloons three days after the party. "Why don't you go on and get to work, and we'll wrap up here?"

Sophie didn't look at Daddy at all as she led the group out into the hall.

"We're right back where we started," Fiona said almost before the door was closed.

"And how," Vincent said. There was no big sloppy grin. "We can write whatever we want, but if they don't like it, we don't get to do it."

"I bet your parents aren't like ours," Darbie said to him.

"No," Vincent said. "Mine are worse. The only reason they aren't here is because they're out of town. I'm surprised my father didn't have himself patched in by satellite."

Wow, Sophie thought. *These guys are empathizing all over the place.* "I didn't know boys had these kinds of problems too," she said.

Jimmy nodded shyly, and Nathan turned red.

"Does the phrase 'house arrest' mean anything to you?" Vincent said. "That's the way I feel 99 percent of the time."

Willoughby put one arm around Sophie's shoulders and the other around Darbie's. "My offer is still open," she said. "Ya'll can come to my house anytime you need to escape."

"We don't have time to escape," Fiona said. "We have a film to do. Only I don't see how it's going to be anything close to real now. We might as well do 'The Three Little Pigs' or something."

For the second time that day, they all looked at Sophie. She could feel Goodsy Malone giving her mind a shove. "No," Sophie said. "We just have to stick together and help each other through this."

"Corn Flake Code," Darbie said.

"Huh?" Nathan said.

Fiona gave Darbie a poke. "It's a girl thing," she said to Nathan. And then she turned to Sophie. "You think we can make it real and still follow all their rules?"

Something tickled at the back of Sophie's mind. The image of pinch-faced Pharisees saying, "Look! What you're doing is unlawful!"

"Yes, I do," Sophie said. "And maybe we can convince them that the rules have changed."

They all met after school that day and Friday—all except Willoughby, of course—and tried to recapture the fun they'd been having with Goodsy and the gangsters before the Parent Patrol came in.

But trying to "suggest" a raid on a suspected gang meeting and just "discussing" the bullet holes in the church wall instead of showing how they got there left the group feeling like deflated balloons again.

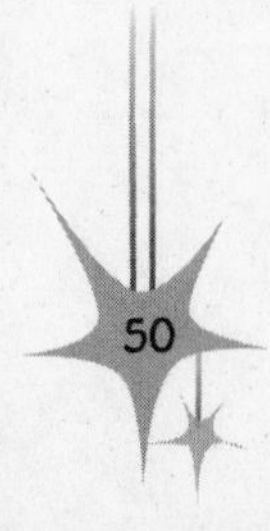

6

The only thing that gave the girls their bounce back was their sleepover at Fiona's Friday night. Kitty was there.

"I can't believe my mom even let me come," she said.

Sophie couldn't either. Kitty's mother had made Miss Odetta, Boppa's new wife, promise to call her if Kitty so much as hiccuped. Miss Odetta, who was one of Fiona's former nannies (the one who had given demerits for breaking the tiniest rules) was now officially part of the Parent Patrol.

Everyone started to sag.

"Okay," Sophie said, "I have an idea."

"Unless it's deadly dull, we probably can't use it," Fiona said.

"No!" Sophie squatted in front of Kitty's wheelchair. "We can show

how heinous the gangsters were without really being violent. We'll show them kidnapping a poor sick helpless girl in a wheelchair and holding her hostage — but not hurting her."

"I can play helpless!" Kitty said.

A slow smile smoothed the frown from Fiona's face. "Now that is the ant's underwear," she said.

When the Lucky Charms and Willoughby arrived Saturday morning, they gave the official "Swell" to the idea, and they all started to work. They discovered along the way that if they used Nathan's twenties slang whenever something rough was called for, and said it out the sides of their mouths, it worked just as well as swearing. Words like *lousy* and *rotten* took on a whole new meaning. "Bushwa!" and "Gadzooks!" were by far the best.

By the time Boppa offered to treat them all to ice cream, they had an entire parent-safe script written.

"Y'know," Darbie said when they'd all piled into the big Ford Expedition, "I think it would be the bee's knees if we used our new language in our emails and IMs."

"Did you just say 'the bee's knees'?" Boppa said from the driver's seat. He smiled his soft Boppa-smile. "My father used to say that."

"Rats," Fiona whispered as they pulled into the Baskin-Robbins parking lot. Out loud she said, before he could open the locks, "Boppa, why don't you just give me the money, and I'll bring yours out to you?"

There was a tiny pause before the locks clicked and doors flew open. Sophie caught a glimpse of Boppa's caterpillar eyebrows in the rearview mirror. They had a sad droop to them.

"I feel kind of bad leaving him in the car," Sophie said to Fiona as they hurried across the parking lot. "I mean, he's Boppa!"

"How else are we ever going to have a private conversation?" Fiona said. She stopped at the door, a wad of Boppa's money

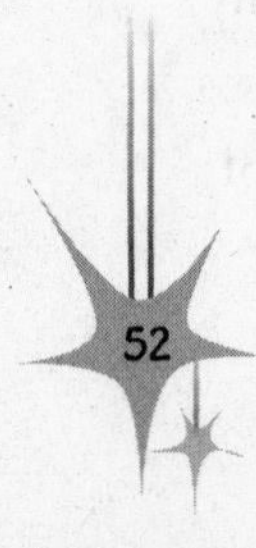

rolled up in her hand. "Nobody on the Parent Patrol is going to *let* us grow up. We just have to *do* it."

Sophie held back as Fiona went inside, and she imagined the kind eyes.

We aren't doing something wrong, are we? she said silently. *Don't the rules have to change so we can grow up?*

There was no answer. But for a crazy moment, Sophie thought she saw Jesus' eyebrows drooping.

When Sophie, Darbie, and Fiona got to first period Monday morning, Mrs. Clayton was standing in the hallway with Jimmy, bullet eyes looking ready to fire. For a second, Sophie wondered if Jimmy had tried "bushwa" on her already.

"Sophie," Mrs. Clayton said, "I need to talk to you too." She nodded to Darbie and Fiona to go on into the room. "Round Table tomorrow during lunch," she continued when Fiona had craned her neck as long as she could and disappeared through the doorway. "We have an interesting case this time."

"Gadzooks!" Sophie said.

"Excuse me?" Mrs. Clayton said.

Jimmy shuffled his feet. "She means — "

"I think I know what she means. I'm just not sure it's — well, whatever."

Mrs. Clayton was still shaking her cement hair-helmet as Sophie and Jimmy went inside.

"It works," Sophie whispered.

"And how," Jimmy whispered back.

"Don't forget, you two," Mrs. Clayton said from behind them. "Don't listen to any rumors about this case."

There were definitely plenty of them not to listen to. By the time Sophie got to third period, she'd heard everything from somebody stealing a teacher's grade book to someone tossing a substitute out a second-story window. The Corn Pops were responsible for most of that, Sophie was sure. They passed notes all through the two-hour English and history block.

The only story Sophie believed came from Willoughby. She cornered Sophie when Coach Yates sent them to the closet for basketballs.

"I know who's going to Round Table," Willoughby said. "They're my friends, and I need you to help them."

She was twirling a curl so tightly around her finger this time, Sophie was sure the end would pop off.

"What friends?" Sophie said. "None of the Flakes — "

"Not ya'll," Willoughby said. She pulled Sophie farther into the closet by her sweatshirt sleeve. "It's two of my cheerleader friends. I really need you to make sure they don't get any after-school punishment, or they'll get suspended from the squad for missing practice. Will you — please?"

"What did they do?" Sophie said.

Willoughby spread her hands like fans. "They didn't do anything — "

She stopped, and her eyes widened at something over Sophie's shoulder. When Sophie turned to look, two heads disappeared from the doorway, but not before Sophie saw that they belonged to the two eighth-grade girls on her bus — the ones with the cell phones. Sophie whipped back around to Willoughby, whose eyes were practically begging.

"Them?" Sophie said.

"Victoria and Ginger," Willoughby said. "They're really nice, and there's no way they did anything wrong. Mr. Bentley's just too strict. He doesn't understand anything." Willoughby narrowed her eyes. "He's worse than any of ya'll's parents."

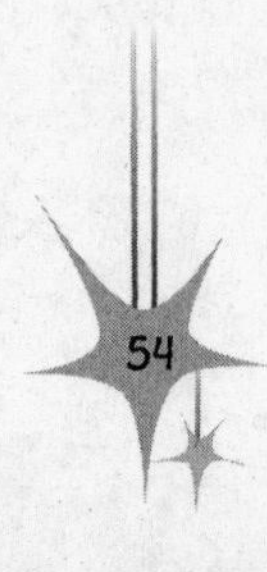

Sophie's stomach squirmed. Mr. Bentley had never sent anybody to Round Table unless he was really sure they needed help with their attitude or something. But Willoughby looked convinced—

"Will you help?" Willoughby said. "I told them we could count on you."

"Where did you go for those basketballs, the factory?"

Sophie had never been glad to hear Coach Yates' voice before, or happy to see her ponytail-pinched face scowling at her.

"Sorry," Sophie said. She grabbed a bag of balls.

She headed for the closet door, dragging the bag. Willoughby tried to follow with another one, but Coach Yates said, "I need to talk to you, Wiley."

Willoughby's face snapped into a smile as if someone were about to take her picture.

"Go start handing those out, LaCroix." Coach Yates waited until Sophie was out of hearing range before she turned to Willoughby, who was still wearing a smile as fakey as the Corn Pops'.

There was no time to tell the other Flakes about any of that before lunchtime, not with a Miss Imes math test fourth period. And Sophie needed to talk to them before her stomach tied into a square knot.

But when the bell rang for lunch, Willoughby was waiting in the doorway to the cafeteria. She hooked her arm around Sophie's and towed her inside—but not toward the Corn Flakes' usual table. Willoughby dragged her past the entire seventh-grade section with Fiona calling, "Gadzooks! Where are you going?" in the background.

"Here she is!" Willoughby said, and thrust Sophie into a chair. She was surrounded by eighth-grade girls, but the only two Sophie really saw were the Cell Phone Twins.

"You must be Sophie," said the very blonde one with the striking blue eyes. "I'm Victoria."

"Oh," Sophie said. She could feel her whole self turning into a very large sore thumb.

"I'm Ginger," said the one who looked like an elf. She put out a thin hand toward Sophie. Sophie stared at it for a long, embarrassing minute before she realized Ginger wanted her to shake it. When she did, it felt like a feather in her palm.

"Haven't I seen you around?" Victoria said. She nudged a cardboard tray of nachos toward Sophie. "Have one."

"You ride my bus," Sophie said. "Or I ride your bus—or something." "That's it." Victoria smiled with the ease of a star on a talk show. "Do you know you have the cutest haircut?"

Ginger nodded as if she were going to grab scissors immediately and try to copy Sophie's 'do on herself.

"She used to be bald," Willoughby said. "She shaved her head for our friend who has cancer."

Sophie waited for the curled lips that usually came after that announcement, but Victoria and Ginger both nodded as if they were in awe.

"When you said she'd do anything for a friend," Ginger said to Willoughby, "you weren't kidding."

Her voice was low and throaty, and nothing much on her moved when she talked. It made Sophie feel like she herself was going to do something spastic any minute. She was afraid to even reach for a nacho.

Victoria leaned forward, so that her blonde hair slipped silkily onto her chest. "Listen," she said. Her blue eyes were serious, like a grown-up's. It occurred to Sophie that she seemed even older than Lacie. "Thanks for helping us tomorrow. We thought once Mr. Bentley got us on his hate list, there was nothing we could do."

"'Til Willoughby told us about you," Ginger said. She put both slender arms, clad tightly in pink, around Willoughby. "We love her."

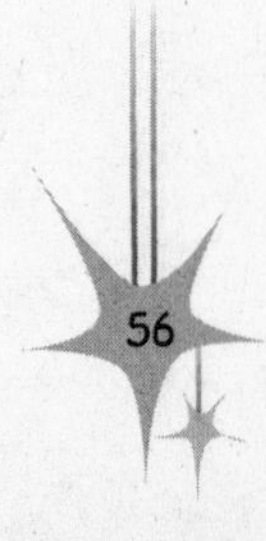

Willoughby smiled until tears sparkled in her eyes. Sophie could feel the knot in her stomach making another loop.

I haven't said I'd help yet! Sophie wanted to scream at Willoughby. *I don't even know what they did. Or didn't do. Or anything!*

But Willoughby was gazing at her as if Sophie had just offered to give her a lifesaving kidney.

"We need to celebrate," Victoria said. She leaned in, and everyone else leaned too. "There's no school Thursday or Friday, so let's have a party Wednesday night."

And then, like someone had just given them a cue, the entire table looked at Willoughby.

"Okay," Willoughby said. "We're out of soda, though."

"Oh, we'll definitely bring more over," Ginger said.

The party's going to be at Willoughby's? Sophie thought. She couldn't have been more confused.

"You come too, Stephi," Victoria said.

"Sophie!" Willoughby said, with a half-poodle-shriek.

"You don't have to bring your own drinks, though," Victoria said to Sophie. She gave her a you're-in-on-the-secret smile. "I figure it's the least we can do."

"You're not eating," Ginger said, inching the nachos closer to Sophie. "Are you trying to keep that cute little figure?"

Sophie looked down at her still-flat chest. Willoughby nudged her.

"See?" she said. "I told you they were nice." She rolled her eyes. "There's no way they would ever give Coach Yates attitude."

"Is that what—," Sophie said.

Willoughby gave a little poodle-yelp. "That's like something Julia and them would do."

Victoria froze with a dripping chip halfway to her lips. "Those little princess wannabes?" she said.

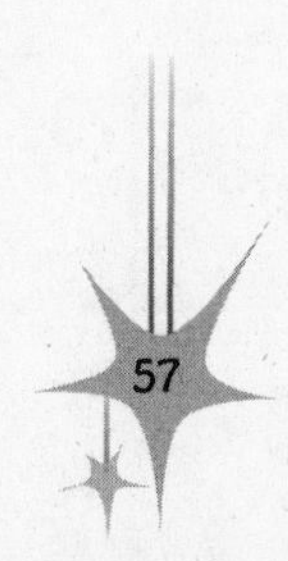

There was unanimous disgust around the table.

"No way we're like them," Ginger said.

For the first time, Sophie found herself nodding. Maybe, just maybe ... if these girls saw the Corn Pops for what they were, they might actually be as nice as Willoughby said.

They haven't put me down one time since I've been at the table, she thought. *Corn Pop Julia couldn't get through one nacho without making me feel like I'm a piece of lint —*

"I want to know how you got up the courage to shave your head," Victoria said. She was smiling right into Sophie. "That was so brave."

Squinting suspiciously, Sophie focused hard on Victoria. When one of the Corn Pops was being *that* nice to her, she could smell the fake factor. But Victoria actually looked impressed. It was worth checking out —

"Kitty's my friend," Sophie said. "I didn't want her to be all alone." Now came the final test. "Wouldn't you do the same for Ginger?"

Victoria's eyes widened, as if she were surprised. Then slowly she looked at Ginger, and she bit her glossy lip. "I think I would," she said. And then she gave Ginger a hug.

By the time lunch was over, Sophie was thinking things like Victoria and Ginger couldn't have committed the sin of back-talking to a teacher. And after all, Coach Yates *had* been grumpier than usual lately. Even Coach Virile had said so.

So the next day at the Round Table meeting, Sophie did her best Goodsy Malone–like defense of Victoria Peyton and Ginger Jenkins before they even came in.

"Sounds like a case of misunderstanding," she told the council. "This can be worked out, see? We don't need to bring in the big guns. Just a sit-down-and-talk. With a neutral party present." She turned to Coach Virile and wished she were wearing a fedora so she could push it back for dramatic effect. "Somebody like Coach here."

Mrs. Clayton looked around the table. "Anyone else?"

"Sure, whatever," said Hannah. She was the eighth-grade girl on the council, a serious brunette with contact lenses that always seemed to bother her. She blinked rapidly at Oliver, the eighth-grade boy. "Sounds like she had it all figured out before we even got here."

Oliver plucked at the rubber band on his braces and nodded.

Miss Imes' eyebrows were aimed at her forehead, but Coach Virile nodded. "I think it's worth a try. I can meet them — "

"How about during lunch tomorrow?" Sophie said.

"It's big of you to arrange Coach Nanini's schedule for him, Sophie." Mrs. Clayton's voice was flat.

"It's okay," Coach said. "I'll set it up with Coach Yates."

Sophie tried not to make her long, relieved breath too obvious. Victoria and Ginger wouldn't miss any practice. Willoughby would be happy.

And I upheld the Corn Flake Code of loyalty, Sophie thought.

It was the bee's knees.

7

Not everybody was as happy with Sophie as Willoughby was.

"Don't I know you?" Fiona said when Sophie sat down next to her in fifth-period science. "Didn't you used to eat lunch with us?"

"I had Round Table today," Sophie said. "And yesterday – "

"You were helping Willoughby. I get that." Fiona lowered her voice as the bell rang. "I'm just missing you. And Willoughby. Why's she all about those eighth graders now? What's wrong with *us*?"

Darbie leaned over from the desk on the other side of Sophie. "We've got bigger problems than that," she said. She looked at Fiona. "Did you tell her?"

"Tell me what?"

"Mr. Stires called an emergency Film Club meeting while you and Jimmy were at Round Table," Fiona said. "He and Miss Imes emailed our script to all the parents, and somebody said they thought the kidnapping scene was too 'scary' for kids our age."

"That's our best scene!" Sophie wailed, loud enough for Mr. Stires to look up from taking roll and twitch his mustache.

"Mr. Stires wouldn't tell us who complained," Fiona whispered.

He didn't have to, Sophie thought. She would have bet her video camera it was her father. It made her want to take a bite right out of her science book.

"Let's head to the lab, folks," Mr. Stires said.

But Sophie couldn't keep her mind on test tubes or anything else except how *un*-swell their film was going to be now.

The whole Film Club gathered just outside the door to sixth-period Life Skills before the bell rang. Maggie kept an eye on the clock so they could dive inside the room in time to escape a tardy-detention from Coach Yates. Her mood hadn't gotten any better in the last few days.

"We have to figure something out," Vincent said. "What's everybody doing after school?"

"Bible study," Maggie said.

"What about after that?"

"We don't have school tomorrow," Darbie said. "Let's meet at my house tonight."

Willoughby was already tugging at Sophie's sleeve, and Sophie knew why.

"This is an emergency," Sophie said to her.

"But you said you'd come," Willoughby said. "I asked you first."

"What are you two going on about?" Darbie said.

Fiona folded her arms and looked at Sophie. "Let me guess. You and Willoughby have plans with those eighth graders."

"Sort of," Sophie said.

"That was a yes-or-no question," Vincent said.

Why do you always have to be so mathematical? Sophie wanted to say to him.

"I did promise Willoughby I'd come to her party," she said.

All Corn Flake eyes shifted to Willoughby.

"You're having a party?" Fiona said.

"I hope this doesn't sound rude, Willoughby," Darbie said. "But why didn't you invite us? We're your best friends."

"Why can't they come?" Sophie knew her voice sounded as fakey as a Corn Pop smile. "It's your house."

Willoughby grabbed a curl and strangled a finger with it. "I kind of already asked them, but they just want Sophie. I mean, they haven't met the rest of you yet."

"So let me get this straight," Fiona said, hands on hips. "*You're* having a party at *your* house, but somebody else is telling you who can come and who can't."

"Yates Alert," Maggie whispered hoarsely. "We have fifteen seconds."

But nobody moved until Willoughby finally nodded and said, "Sort of."

"That was another yes-or-no question," Vincent said.

This time, Sophie had to agree with him.

Maggie herded them all into the room just as the bell rang. There was a note on Sophie's desk almost before Coach Yates closed the door.

"PLEASE come to my party, Sophie," Willoughby had written. "I NEED you there."

Sophie looked over to see tears threatening to spill out onto Willoughby's cheeks.

"I have to go to Willoughby's party," Sophie wrote to Fiona. "I don't know why. I just do."

At Bible study that afternoon, the fact that Kitty was there, tucked neatly into her wheelchair, was overshadowed by Fiona

putting her hand up almost before Dr. Peter could get the words "So, ladies, how was your week?" out of his mouth.

"I guess I'm about to find out," he said, eyes sparkling.

"I just have a question," Fiona said. "What happens if you make a rule and somebody breaks it because there's another rule that is the opposite of that rule?"

Dr. Peter let his eyes cross. It would have been funny if Sophie hadn't known exactly where Fiona was going.

"I'm glad you asked that, actually," Dr. Peter said. "Because it goes back to the story we're studying. Let me ask you something — what did you do Sunday after church?"

They all looked at each other.

"Homework," Gill said.

Harley grunted in agreement.

Maggie was flipping back through her calendar. "We worked on our film," she said.

"It scares me that you have an appointment book, Maggie," Dr. Peter said. "But that's exactly my point. All of you broke the commandment about keeping the Sabbath holy."

"Sorry," Kitty said. And then she gave her nervous Kitty-giggle.

Sophie squirmed a little. "But I thought that's what the story was about. Didn't Jesus change that rule because his disciples were hungry?"

Dr. Peter rubbed his hands together and wrinkled his glasses into place with his nose. "Just as I thought. We need to look at the story a little more closely." He picked up a stack of pastel-colored pads and handed them out, each one matching a beanbag chair color. Kitty giggled and said she'd missed this class *so* much. Sophie just got a squirmy feeling in her stomach. So far this didn't promise to help her with the Corn Flake situation, much less Daddy and the Parent Patrol.

"On this pad," Dr. Peter said, "I want you to write down all the rules you are expected to follow, even the ones you've made for your own group of friends."

"Corn Flake Code," Maggie said.

Gill looked at Harley. "Do we have rules?"

Harley, of course, grunted.

It took the whole hour for everybody to list all their rules, since naturally they had to talk about every one as they went along. By the end of the class, Sophie was no closer to any answers. In fact, the chain around her ankle had gained several links. Dr. Peter said he'd explain it all next week. Fiona was still saying things to Sophie like, "I get it, but I don't get it. Gadzooks!"

Sophie had no word, even in their new slang, to describe how she felt going over to Willoughby's that night.

I want to go, but I don't, she thought in Daddy's truck on the way over. *I'm happy they asked me, and I'm not. I want to help Willoughby, but I don't want to hurt my other Corn Flakes.*

"You look like you're having a scrimmage with yourself over there, Soph," Daddy said. "Want me to referee?"

His eyes were actually sympathetic, but even as Sophie opened her mouth to explain it to him, she could hear Fiona saying, *Somebody said they thought the kidnapping scene was too "scary" for kids our age.*

Daddy doesn't even know anything about kids our age, Sophie thought. So what was the point?

Goodsy Malone shook her head. These old town council members, they didn't know from nothin'. She'd have to handle this on her own, just like always.

She settled back into the seat of the 1928 Pierce-Arrow car and watched through the windshield with trained eyes. Even now there could be members of the Capone organization lurking in the shadows. In fact, didn't she see movement in that yard? Wasn't there someone running straight for the Pierce-Arrow?

"Look out!" she shouted, hand already on her weapon.

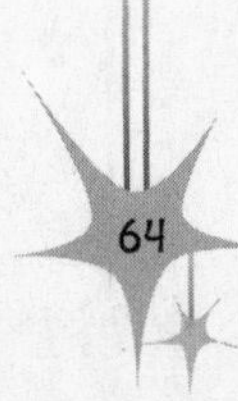

The tires squealed, and the vehicle fishtailed to a stop.

Daddy was glaring at her. "What was that all about?"

Sophie blinked through her glasses at the empty road in front of them.

"Don't be screaming like that when I'm driving," Daddy said as he shook his head and jerked the truck back into gear. "I could have had an accident."

His eyes weren't sympathetic anymore.

Daddy waited in the truck until Willoughby let Sophie in the front door. Sophie wondered if Victoria's and Ginger's parents still did that with them.

"I'm glad he's met your dad before," Sophie said, "or he would have come all the way to the door to check him out."

Willoughby gave a poodle-shriek. "I'm glad he didn't! My dad's at work."

Sophie felt the stomach knot forming again. "He's not gonna be here?"

"No, but it's cool," Willoughby said. "He doesn't care if I have friends over."

Sophie gazed at her in awe.

"Okay, squirt, we're out of here." A curly-haired boy of about eighteen followed his deep voice into the room. There was another identical boy right behind him. He messed up Willoughby's hair with his fingers.

"These are my twin brothers," Willoughby said, "Matt and Andy." She wriggled away from the one with his hands in her hair. "And *fortunately*, they're leaving too."

"Make sure you clean up after your party," one of them said.

"By eleven. Dad gets off at midnight," the other one said.

"I know, I know," Willoughby said.

Hands-in-the-Hair waved his cell phone at her as the two of them went out the front door.

"I *know*!" Willoughby said. She rolled her eyes at Sophie. "They're way worse than anybody's parents."

Then why are they leaving? Sophie thought. Her stomach was knotted up tight enough to hold a yacht in place. It was the first time she'd ever been alone in somebody else's house without an adult there. *Not* being in that situation was one of the things she'd written on her rules list that very day in Bible study.

I don't think Jesus would like this, she thought. *Much less Mama and Daddy.*

But before she could mention that to Willoughby, the doorbell rang. Willoughby yelped, and the house was suddenly full of eighth-grade girls.

Sophie recognized some of them from the lunch table the day before, but there were at least ten more besides them. All of them looked like they shopped, had their hair cut and colored, and took modeling classes at the same place. Sophie felt more flat-chested and less Goodsy Malone–confident by the second.

Until Victoria parted the crowd and made a beeline for her.

"Stephi!" she said.

"It's actually Sophie," Sophie said.

"I know, but I like calling you Stephi. You remind me of my cousin Stephanie—you both look adorable in glasses. Come on, I want Ginger to give you a manicure. She's amazing. Have you ever had one?"

"No," Sophie said as she trailed her to Willoughby's family room. *Wait 'til she sees I don't even have any nails.*

But Ginger, who had a full manicure set spread out on the coffee table, didn't even blink when she saw Sophie's gnawed-off absence of fingernails.

"I'm going to put fake nails on you," she said. "They'll be fabulous."

Next to Sophie on the couch, somebody else was getting a pedicure, and on the floor, three girls were pulling DVDs out

of their purses. Sophie started to relax. This really wasn't that much different from the Corn Flake sleepovers —

Until a DVD was popped into the player, and a big *R* appeared on the TV screen.

Sophie tried not to let her eyes pop out. She'd never seen an R-rated movie in her life. That too had been on her rule list.

Victoria swept into the room holding a Diet Dr. Pepper in one hand and positioning the fingers of the other one like she was holding a telephone. "Willoughby!" she called out. "Where's your cell phone?"

Where's yours? Sophie thought as Willoughby tucked her little pink phone into Victoria's hand.

"I get it after you," Ginger said to Victoria. She pressed a shiny squared-off nail onto Sophie's finger and held it up to survey it, frowning. "Too big. You're so petite." She pulled it off. "Parents are so clueless."

"Why are they clueless this time?" said Giving-a-Pedicure.

"I *told* them that Round Table making us have a talk with Coach Nanini wasn't a punishment," Ginger said, "but do they get that? No. They took my cell phone for three days."

"Call Child Protective Services," Getting-a-Pedicure said.

Sophie looked at her quickly to make sure she was kidding.

"Here," Victoria said, tossing the phone to Ginger. "I'll finish Stephi's nails."

"Did you get him?" Ginger said as she poked out a number.

"I had to leave him a text message," Victoria said. "These are darling on you, Stephi." She wiggled her eyebrows up at Ginger. "He'll be here."

He? Sophie thought. *Here?*

"Okay, listen to this." A willowy girl curled up in Willoughby's father's recliner and held up a magazine. "Here's a quiz: 'Are You a Boy Magnet?' "

"Who in here needs to take that quiz?" Victoria said. "We all have boyfriends." She looked at Sophie, who was trying to will herself to disappear under the sofa. "Do you?"

"Uh, no," Sophie said.

"Why not?" said Giving-a-Pedicure. "You're too cute to be single."

"It's because seventh-grade boys are still such babies," Ginger said. She tossed the phone back to Victoria and took over the last of Sophie's press-on manicure. "You need an eighth-grade boy, Sophia."

Sophie didn't even attempt to correct her. She knew nothing would come out but a squeak. An eighth-grade boy? *EWW!*

"We'll get you any guy you want," Ginger said to her. "As long as he isn't already taken."

"What about Scottie Fischer?" Getting-a-Pedicure said.

Ginger studied Sophie. "They would be cute together. Want us to fix you up?"

Yes—to a truck—and drag me out of here! That definitely sounded better than all of this right now. Sophie almost melted into a relief-puddle when the doorbell rang. Ginger dashed for the door with Getting-a-Pedicure behind her, gauze still stuffed between her toes.

But when Sophie saw half the Great Marsh Middle School boys' basketball team stream into the family room, she ran like a rabbit to the kitchen in search of Willoughby—who was nowhere to be found.

Sophie launched herself at a cooler full of sodas just for something to do while she thought about how she was going to escape. She hadn't put the rule about not hanging out with boys without any adults present on her list. It hadn't even come up in her life yet.

Ginger came in then, draped around a tall boy who looked like he shaved already. Sophie wriggled past them with a Sprite and darted for the stairs to the second floor.

"What's that little seventh grader doing here?" she heard the boy say.

"Shut up. She's valuable," Ginger said.

I'm valuable? Sophie thought. *What—like a bank account or something?*

Suddenly, she didn't feel like a Boy Magnet with a cute little figure and fabulous fake nails. Parking the Sprite on the steps, she headed for Willoughby's room, where she knew there was a house phone. The only thing to do right now was call Fiona and find out what to do. Gadzooks.

"Bunting residence," said the voice on the other end.

Sophie held back a groan. It was Miss Odetta.

"May I speak with Fiona?" she said.

Something beeped in her ear, and for a minute, Sophie thought Miss Odetta had hung up.

"Is this Sophie?" Miss Odetta said, in that voice she used when somebody was about to get a demerit.

"Yes, ma'am," Sophie said. "May I speak with Fiona?"

There was another beep. "What is wrong with this phone?" Miss Odetta said. "This thing does everything but the dishes, and I don't know what any of it means— "

"May I *please* speak to Fiona?" Sophie's voice threatened to squeak out of hearing range.

"She's over at Darbie's house," Miss Odetta said. "Why aren't you there?"

Sophie thanked her and hung up before Miss Odetta could give her a demerit for not being with Fiona.

I deserve one! Sophie thought. *What am I doing* here?

In the distance, another phone rang.

Probably a bunch of high school boys calling on the cell phone to say they're coming over, too, Sophie thought. *I have to get out of here.*

For a crazy moment, she looked at Willoughby's bedroom window. She could always climb out of it and run to Kitty's house, which was only a block away.

But Kitty was probably at Darbie's house too, along with everyone else Sophie felt *safe* with.

The only thing to do now was call home and ask Daddy to come get her. And then she'd have to tell him why—

"Oh, no!" someone screamed from downstairs. Sophie would have recognized that poodle-yelp anywhere. "That was my dad! He got off early!"

Then there was another poodle-cry—a frightened one.

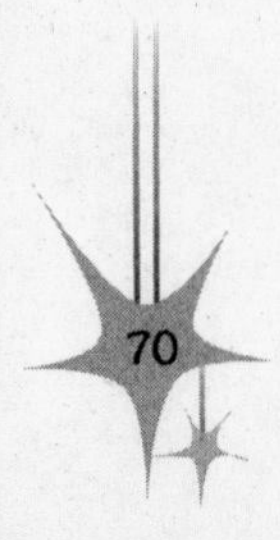

8

In a matter of minutes, Willoughby's house was empty of eighth graders, without even a trace of a press-on nail left behind. Willoughby leaned against the front door and whimpered, "Sophie, please — you have to help me clean up before my father gets home."

Sophie was about to say, *I thought he didn't care if you had a party*, but Willoughby burst into tears.

"What do you want me to do?" Sophie said.

"Make it look like nobody was here but you and me. You take the family room. I have to call my brother."

"Okay, but I don't get it — "

"Sophie please — hurry!"

The fear in Willoughby's voice sent Sophie charging into the family room, where she clanked soda cans into a

garbage bag and sprayed air freshener over the nail glue smell. She was dumping the trash bag into the outside can when she heard a car pull into the driveway. The thought of jumping the fence and running crossed her mind, but Willoughby stuck her head out the back door and said, "He's here!" It sounded like the poodle was drawing her final breath.

The front door opened as Willoughby motioned for Sophie to sit on one of the snack bar stools while she herself stuck her head in the refrigerator.

"I wish Matt would hurry up with the milk," she said into its depths. "I'm dying for a milk shake."

"Matt went out?" said a deep voice from the doorway.

Sophie flinched, nearly falling off the stool. She'd heard Willoughby's father talk before, but she'd never noticed him growling like a German shepherd. The way he took inventory of the kitchen with his eyes made Sophie wish she had jumped the fence after all, and taken Willoughby with her.

"I just went out to get some milk," said another voice. One of the twins appeared in the doorway with two gallon jugs and a grin—a very shaky grin.

"How long were you gone?" Mr. Wiley snarled at him.

Two hours! Sophie thought.

"Not that long," Matt said. "I knew if I didn't get right back with the stuff, Will was going to go into milk shake withdrawal."

Willoughby pulled her head out of the refrigerator and put out her hands for the milk jugs. "You're a lifesaver," she said to Matt.

Sophie was sure she wasn't talking about milk shakes.

Sophie couldn't even drink the one Willoughby fixed and carried upstairs for her. Her stomach was nothing *but* a knot.

Willoughby flopped down on her bed and covered her face with her hands. "That was close," she said. "Somebody must

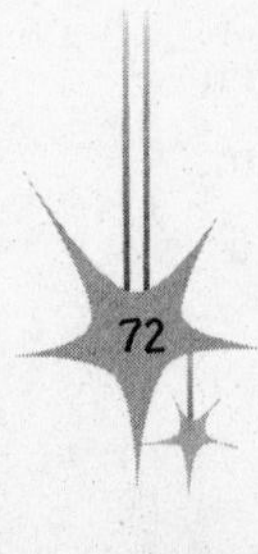

have been on our phone when he called. Don't they know about call waiting?" She peeked out through her fingers. "It's a good thing he tried me on my cell."

Sophie perched uneasily on the edge of a white wicker chair. "What would have happened if he'd caught all those kids here?"

"He would have yelled at Matt and Andy," she said. "They aren't supposed to leave me alone when I have a friend over." Willoughby sat up. "They really wanted to go out, and I really wanted to have this party, so we worked out a plan. I hate that they almost got in trouble. They're cool brothers."

Matt wasn't acting cool just now, Sophie thought. *I think he was scared to death.*

"Aren't you going to drink that?" Willoughby pointed to Sophie's milk shake. Her hand trembled.

"You okay?" Sophie said.

Willoughby plastered on a smile, the same too-cheerful one she'd used with Coach Yates. "I am now. It was worth it, though. Wasn't that a cool party?" She twirled a curl. "I hope Victoria and them had a good time."

Sophie ran a hand over her own short crop of hair. A fake nail hung up in it. "Would they still be worth it if Matt got in trouble?"

"Are you kidding me?" Willoughby's face sobered as she looked at Sophie. "Victoria and Ginger told me they think I have what it takes to be captain of the eighth-grade squad next year. And since they're cocaptains this year, they get to be judges when we have tryouts in March. You know what that means?"

"No," Sophie said.

"It means I'm practically guaranteed to make it!"

"But you're the best," Sophie said. "You'd make it anyway."

Willoughby shook her head, sending the curls into a frenzy. "When you get up into *eighth* grade, it gets tougher. It pays to have somebody on your side."

The Corn Flakes are on your side, Sophie wanted to say. But she wasn't sure that would make any difference to Willoughby right now. She had Victoria-worship shining on her face.

"I'm getting my pajamas on," Sophie said.

"Just one thing, Soph," Willoughby said as Sophie reached for her backpack. "Would you please not tell your parents about what happened tonight?"

Sophie pretended to have trouble with the zipper while her mind spun.

This feels like lying. Willoughby's too good at lying.

But what good would it do to tell her parents and get Matt in trouble?

Not to mention herself.

She knew she should have called home the minute she found out Willoughby's dad wasn't home. She also knew that Willoughby was waiting for her answer with fear flickering in her eyes.

She's that afraid for Matt to get yelled at?

There was something else going on, something that made Sophie want to run to Mama and whisper to her about the frightened squeal in Willoughby's voice and the fear-flickers in her eyes.

"It's Corn Flake Code," Willoughby said. "We all promised we'd help each other with our parent stuff."

"You said you didn't have parent stuff," Sophie said.

Willoughby rolled her eyes. "It's not my parent stuff. It's Matt's. When you don't have a mom, you get way close to your brothers. We protect each other."

"From what?" Sophie said.

"Just promise me, Sophie," Willoughby said. She rolled her eyes again, but Sophie knew that this time she was trying to roll away tears.

"Okay," Sophie said. "But I can't come over here when your dad's not home anymore. You *couldn't* protect me from what my parents would say if they knew."

"You have my word." Willoughby flew to the chair and threw her arms around Sophie. "I love you, Corn Flake," she said.

I love you too, Sophie thought later. She sat up in bed, peeling off the phony fingernails while Willoughby slept beside her. *But I don't know if what I just promised was such a good thing.*

Sophie shivered and closed her eyes. Jesus was right there with his kind ones.

Are you disappointed in me? she prayed to him. *I hope not, because I'm really confused, and I really need your help.* She sighed into the pillow. *I really need you to show me what the rules are.*

The Film Club spent most of their long-weekend days together working on their movie. Willoughby missed a lot of rehearsal time because she said she had cheerleading stuff.

Sophie wondered whether she was talking about the seventh-grade squad, or the eighth-grade.

They filmed all the movie except for the kidnapping scene. They were gathered in the sunroom at the back of Kitty's house trying to figure out what to do about what the Parent Patrol had said, when there was a tap on the glass.

"It's Willoughby!" Kitty said.

"I hope she has the pictures for what we're supposed to do with our hair," Fiona said. "She's giving about 50 percent, which is *not* what we all promised."

Kitty ignored her and pushed open the door, letting in a blast of cold late-November air. "Come in before you freeze to death!"

But Willoughby stood in the doorway, shivering and shaking her head. Sophie saw the flicker in her eyes, and she herself started to shake.

"I just need to talk to Sophie," Willoughby said. "In private."

Sophie felt Fiona stiffen beside her.

Throwing her jacket around her shoulders, Sophie slipped outside to join Willoughby. She heard Fiona say in her twenties voice, "What are the rest of us? Chopped liver?"

Willoughby grabbed Sophie's jacket sleeve and dragged her around the side of the house. She was breathing so hard, little puffs of frosty air were coming out of her nose.

"Are you in trouble?" Sophie said. "Did your dad find out—"

"It's not about me," Willoughby said. Her already-big eyes got bigger. "It's Victoria and Ginger."

"Again?" Sophie said. She hoped Willoughby didn't see her sagging with relief.

"They might have to go before the Round Table again."

"Okay," Sophie said. "You know that's not a punishment, even if their parents—"

"You have to say that they were at my house all Wednesday night."

Sophie knew she would have frozen even if the icy wind weren't whipping through her.

"But they weren't," she said.

"They were there part of the time. I really need you to do this, Sophie. Please—"

"Willoughby!"

Even from a block away, the voice was loud and deep and had a growl in it.

"That's my dad—I have to go," Willoughby said.

And she ran as if Al Capone's entire mob were after her.

"I can't lie for them!" Sophie called after her.

But she knew Willoughby didn't hear her as her father growled again. "Willoughby, get home!"

It definitely didn't sound like it was Matt he was mad at.

When Sophie went back into the house, everyone had left the sunroom except Fiona, who was "up to ninety," as Darbie would say.

"What's going on?" Fiona said.

Sophie swallowed hard. The tangle of rules seemed to be caught in her throat. "Willoughby wants me to do something I can't do, and I didn't get to tell her I couldn't do it because her father yelled at her."

"I thought she had Superfather," Fiona said. "What is going *on*?"

"I'll tell you after I talk to Willoughby."

Fiona's gray eyes went into slits. "Why do I have to wait? I'm your best friend."

"Because I don't know which rule I'm supposed to be following!" Sophie said.

Fiona looked closely at her. "You're about to freak out."

"And how," Sophie said. One thing she *did* know, though: the reason she was now so valuable to the eighth graders.

She wanted to email Willoughby as soon as she got home, but Lacie was on the computer, moaning about the huge history paper she was "never going to finish."

Sophie tried calling the Wiley house, but when one of the twins answered the phone, he told her Willoughby couldn't come to the phone and hung up before Sophie could ask him when she could. She imagined his lips trembling the way they had Wednesday night.

Please help me with all these rules, she begged Jesus when she went to bed. *I need to know what to do!*

One rule was very clear: she couldn't lie for Victoria and Ginger. It was one thing to keep a secret for Willoughby, and another to tell a big old whopper for girls she didn't even know — girls who said things like, "She's valuable," even if they also said Sophie was cute and a boy magnet.

As she thought about that during first period, she watched Colton Messik saunter to the pencil sharpener and do a fake burp in Anne-Stuart's ear as he passed.

EWW.

"Sophie," said a trumpet-voice at her elbow.

Sophie looked up at Mrs. Clayton.

"Round Table during lunch today. We have some repeaters."

Sophie felt her stomach harden.

It was still in a mass of knots when she and Jimmy got to the council room and joined Hannah and Oliver and Coach Virile, Mrs. Clayton, Miss Imes, and Coach Yates. Sophie didn't see how Coach Yates' face could be any more pinched-in. She was starting to look like a Pharisee.

"It's those cheerleaders again," Hannah whispered to Sophie and Jimmy while the teachers talked to each other in under-the-breath voices. She blinked about two hundred times. "No offense, Sophie, but I didn't think a little chat with Coach Nanini was going to change them."

"Let's come to order," Mrs. Clayton said. "I want us to talk before we bring our offenders in." Her eyebrows pointed. "I think you'll all remember Victoria Peyton and Ginger Jenkins, who were before us last week for a confrontation they had with Coach Yates. Any further problems, Coach?"

Coach Yates shook her head. "They've basically been avoiding me."

"At least they have *some* brains," Oliver muttered.

"They're coming before us again today," Mrs. Clayton went on, "about a different matter. It seems that they were seen out after curfew on Wednesday night, which means Ms. Barnes, the eighth-grade squad coach, has suspended them from the cheerleading squad for two weeks."

"The end of life as they know it," Hannah said.

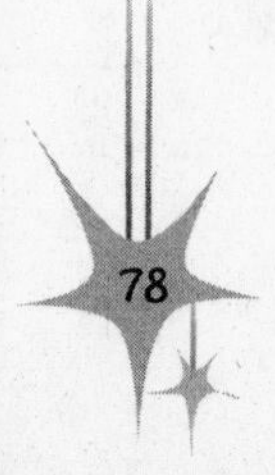

Mrs. Clayton shot her a bullet-look. "Let's try to keep our personal feelings out of this."

Oliver strummed the rubber band on his braces. "Who saw them out after curfew?"

"What difference does that make?" Hannah said.

"Could be somebody that wants to frame them. That would make it more interesting."

"That would be fascinating," Mrs. Clayton said dryly, "except that it was a reliable source, and no one has come forward to provide them with an alibi."

"There was one attempt," Miss Imes put in. "But that was an unsigned note."

Unsigned by Willoughby, Sophie thought. That definitely wasn't Corn Flake Code, and it made Sophie homesick for the old Willoughby of before-Victoria-and-Ginger days.

Jimmy raised his hand. "So if they've already gotten a punishment, why are they coming here?"

"Because we're about helping kids become better than they are," Coach Virile said. "And after working with these girls just one time, I could see they needed some guidance." His big face softened. "It's not too late."

"Ms. Barnes wants them to have some Round Table rehab before she lets them back on the squad," Mrs. Clayton said. "So let's bring them in and make our recommendation."

Ginger and Victoria both smiled at Sophie when they came in and took their seats as if they were about to be offered the title of cheerleading cocaptains for the rest of their lives.

Sophie considered asking for a restroom pass. But that wasn't something Goodsy Malone would do.

Goodsy narrowed her eyes at the both of them. There were kids who needed help, see, and then there were lyin' little flapper girls

who didn't care about nothin' or nobody. They used people up and then tossed 'em aside like—like yesterday's garbage, see—

Willoughby wasn't yesterday's garbage.

And neither was she.

"Ladies, you know why you're here," Mrs. Clayton said.

"I assume it's to tell us we're not suspended," Victoria said.

Sophie watched Miss Imes' eyebrows shoot up, while Coach Nanini's unibrow lowered almost to his nose.

"Wherever did you get that idea?" Mrs. Clayton said.

Victoria's eyes flicked to Sophie. Ginger's had never left Sophie's face.

Sophie adjusted her glasses and looked back at them. She saw her answer dawn on them and freeze their faces.

"We are here to offer you some help," Coach Nanini said. "Council?"

Sophie raised her hand. "I recommend that we give you Campus Commission after school," she said. "It'll really teach you a lot. You know"—Sophie drilled her eyes right into Victoria—"like not to use people."

The teachers all looked puzzled. Ginger and Victoria didn't.

Sophie barely got to her locker after they adjourned before Willoughby was there. Her face was a furious red, and her big eyes looked ready to lunge from her face, right at Sophie.

"You said you'd help!" she said. The poodle voice was out of control.

"No, I didn't," Sophie said.

"Yes, you did. You stood right here in this very spot and said we all had to be loyal to each other, no matter what!" Willoughby stomped her foot. "If what you just did to me is what you mean by loyal, then I don't want to be a Corn Flake anymore!"

Then she turned with a squeal of her sneakers and was gone.

9

By sixth period that day, it was final. Willoughby had officially dropped out of Film Club.

"How much revising will you have to do on your film, then?" Miss Imes said when Sophie and Fiona gave her the news after school. "You only have two weeks left."

Sophie hadn't even thought about that. She was too busy trying to swallow Willoughby's other decision — that she was no longer a Corn Flake either.

Anybody can play a flapper girl in a movie, Sophie told Jesus on the way home on the bus. *But nobody else can be Willoughby in my life.*

Who else would yelp like a poodle at Sophie's funniness?

Who else could do a cheer every time Sophie got above a C on a math test?

Or twirl a curl around her finger when she got nervous? Or throw her arms around Sophie just because?

Sophie wished just this once Jesus would answer in actual words — just appear in the seat next to her on the bus and tell her how to get Willoughby back.

She closed her eyes and imagined him looking kindly, sadly at her. It occurred to her that Willoughby needed to be imagining him right now too. Because unless doing what he wanted her to do became more important than what Victoria and Ginger wanted her to do, things were going to stay just the way they were. Somehow that thought added more weight to that chain around her ankle.

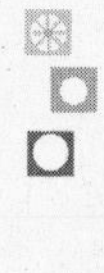

Going home didn't help at all. Daddy was there, white-faced with the news that Mama was going to have to stay in bed until Baby Girl LaCroix was born.

"Four *months*?" Lacie said.

"Don't worry, Lace," Daddy said. "You won't have to cook *every* night. There's always McDonald's."

"Can Mama get up to go to the bathroom?" Zeke said.

"Yeah, Z-Boy, she can do that," Daddy told him.

"Is something the matter with the baby?" Sophie said.

Daddy made a not-too-successful attempt at a smile. "No, she's just an eager little rookie. She wants to come out and play now, and she's not ready."

"Does Mama get to take a bath?" Zeke said.

"Yeah, Z."

"So what's the game plan?" Lacie said. "Obviously we're all going to have to help if we don't want the whole place to fall apart."

"We need a chart like Mama made for Kitty's sisters when she was in the hospital," Sophie said.

"Can she still read with me?" Zeke said.

Daddy patted Z's head, eyes on the girls. "Thank you for having that attitude, Lace, Soph." Sophie thought his eyes looked wet. "You two are on the top shelf looking down."

"It's family, Dad," Lacie said. "We all have to take a hit for the team." To Sophie, Lacie's eyes looked wise as she pushed up her sweat-jacket sleeves and said, "Okay, how does tuna salad sound for dinner?"

While Zeke put in his vote for raisins in the salad, Sophie kept watching Lacie—pulling cans out of the pantry, making an out-of-my-way bun out of her ponytail and sticking a pencil through it, giving Zeke the raisins and a measuring cup so he could help.

Why did I ever think Victoria and Ginger seemed older than Lacie? she thought. *Lacie could be, like, their mom right now.*

There must be a difference, she decided, between acting grown up and really being grown up.

"I can chop the celery," she said.

But being a grown-up was harder than it looked. Dinner had to be fixed, cleaned up, and thought up for the next night. Zeke had to be bathed, chased, and read to. Laundry had to be washed and dried and folded, not to mention collected from every corner of Zeke's room to begin with.

It meant coming home right after school and taking over for the ladies from the church who took turns keeping Mama fed and occupied all day so she wouldn't "go bonkers," as she put it.

It also meant missing Film Club just when Sophie really needed to be there. By Tuesday night, only the second day of their no-Mama routine, Sophie not only felt like she had a chain around her ankle, she was convinced it was attached to a wall.

Some of that was because of Daddy. Even though he was super-busy with Mama and Zeke when he was home, he still had a corner of his brain reserved for running Sophie's life.

"How are the grades, Soph?" he asked when she came down to the study to type her English homework. "You're not involved in too many activities, are you, Baby Girl?" he asked when she was still up at 9:30, writing up her science lab. And when she went downstairs to pick up her laundry, he said, "How are you holding up? Can you handle all this?"

Sophie sagged against the dryer, laundry basket on her hip. It was tempting to tell him she felt like she was dragging a ball and chain, especially when his eyes actually got soft and he took the basket from her.

"I know it's tough," he said. "You and Lacie are being champs about it. Mama and I appreciate it, but you have to let me know if it gets to be too much."

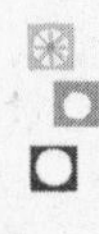

Sophie wanted to leap up for a hang-around-the-neck-legs-dangling Daddy hug—just to feel carefree again for a minute.

But then Daddy said, "After all, you're still a little girl." He passed through the laundry room door with her basket of folded clothes. "By the way, how's that twenties gangster film coming together?"

Sophie got in front of him and pulled the basket out of his hands.

"Fine," she said. She headed for the stairs so she wouldn't add, *No thanks to you*.

"I can take that up for you," he called after her.

"I've got it," she said.

Glasses off and face down in her pink pillow a few minutes later, her thoughts screamed.

Let me get this straight—I have to run the whole house with Lacie and practically give up Film Club so I can raise my baby brother—but I'm still a little girl who can't handle a kidnapping scene where nobody even gets hurt.

I don't get it. I don't get it!

She tried to imagine Jesus, but she wasn't sure just now that she wanted him telling her what to do either. She pawed fitfully at her Bible, but she couldn't remember where the story was that they'd been studying with Dr. Peter.

Dr. Peter.

Sophie felt a spring of hope that bounced her up, but she plopped back down again. Forget Bible study. She had to watch Zeke tomorrow.

And watch life as she knew it disappear.

There was a tap on the door, which Sophie answered with a pillow-muffled grunt.

"Mama wants you to come in and say good night," Daddy said.

Sophie climbed off the bed and hoped she could work up a smile before she got to her parents' room.

Mama held out her arms to Sophie when she arrived and ran her hand down the back of Sophie's head.

"I miss our time together, Dream Girl," she said. "But I know you're busy helping."

"It's okay," Sophie lied.

Mama pushed her back so she could look at her. "Are you sure?"

What am I supposed to say? Sophie thought. She didn't know whether she was expected to be a grown-up or a little girl right now.

Mama was still searching her face with her tired Sophie-brown eyes. "Anything you want to talk about?" she said.

Sophie just shook her head. There was another long look and a pause.

"I'm right here," Mama said. She gave a wispy smile. "More than I want to be. You can still talk to me."

Can I? Sophie thought. She could feel her throat getting thick.

"Just promise me something," Mama said. "Promise that if you can't talk to me or Daddy, you'll at least talk to Dr. Peter."

"I won't even get to see Dr. Peter," Sophie blurted out. "I can't go to Bible study because I have to watch Zeke."

She wanted to chomp her tongue off as Mama's mouth dropped at the corners.

"But it's okay," Sophie said. Her voice squeaked. "It's fine."

"Time for bed, Baby Girl," Daddy said from the doorway.

Sophie escaped to her bedroom, where she cried herself to sleep, because she didn't know what the rules were anymore.

As Sophie boarded the bus the next morning, she spotted Victoria and Ginger, minus their cell phones, sitting in sullen silence on the eighth-grade side. Their eyes looked right through her as if she weren't even there.

It's tough being a law enforcement officer, Goodsy Malone thought as she took her usual watchful position by the window. Not everybody is going to like you, especially those thugs that can't obey the law.

But she didn't have time to think about that right now. She had an invalid girl in a wheelchair to rescue from the lousy Capone men that had nabbed her right out of her house. So far, they hadn't hurt her. At least that was what Goodsy could gather from listening in on the phone calls they let her make to her rich father, mob family leader Shawn O'Banyon. Goodsy had also gathered that the sick girl—Bitsy O'Banyon—was with at least two women. She'd heard their voices in the background during phone calls.

It pays to have a trained ear, is what I say, thought Goodsy. Even now she could detect words she knew she wasn't supposed to hear—

"I don't see why we should keep hanging out with her now," one voice said. "She can't have parties. We can't use her cell phone—"

"And she doesn't have any control over that Stephi girl at all," the other one said. "So what's the point?"

Sophie pressed herself closer to the window. Goodsy didn't have time for eavesdropping. She had mobsters to deal with—

Which she did all day. Goodsy hid behind a literature book during a stakeout — and Sophie nearly blew a quiz on the short story she was supposed to read.

Goodsy put on a disguise so she could spy on Capone — and Sophie got docked points for wearing sunglasses in the gym.

Goodsy checked the addition and subtraction on Al Capone's records, ate lunch in Capone's favorite Italian restaurant, and experimented with bomb-making so she wouldn't be caught by surprise when Capone's men tossed their next one.

By sixth-period Life Skills, Fiona was hoarse from coughing Sophie back on track. Fiona hadn't had to use her come-back-to-the-real-world signal in a long time.

"Are you even here at all today?" she wrote to Sophie in a note while Coach Yates was showing a film.

I don't know, Sophie thought.

Because no matter how deeply she escaped into Goodsy Malone's world, her own world was still the same chained-up, knotted-together mess when she returned to it.

Willoughby still wasn't speaking to the Corn Flakes, or even looking at them.

Their film still wasn't done, and there was no time for Sophie to work on it.

Mama was still in bed so Baby Girl LaCroix wouldn't make a too-early entrance into the world.

Daddy was still treating her like a little girl, unless he needed her to be Zeke's mom or run the dishwasher.

The rules that had once made her life so easy to live were all over in a corner of her mind, arguing with each other.

And the people who used to be there to untie the knots were now out of reach, especially Dr. Peter.

"It's Boppa's turn to drive us to Bible study today," Fiona said when she and Sophie and Maggie and Darbie were at their

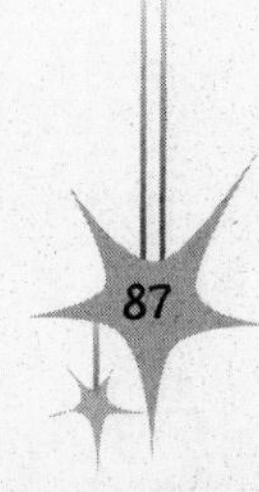

lockers after school. "I hope he doesn't play that elevator music the whole way."

"It's better than Aunt Emily's 'oldies,'" Darbie said. "I'd like to hear some 'newies' once in a while, but she thinks it's all evil or something—"

"I'm not going," Sophie said.

"No way," Maggie said.

"Yes, way. I have to watch Zeke."

"Bushwa!" Fiona said. She linked her arm through Sophie's as the four of them headed for the front of the school.

"Who else is going to do it?" Sophie said.

"Boppa," Maggie said.

"What?"

"Boppa," Maggie said again. Sophie followed her pointing finger to the Expedition parked at the curb. Boppa was behind the wheel, and Zeke was in the second seat, yakking away.

"All aboard," Boppa said through the rolled-down window. "First stop, church. Next stop, Bunting's Day Care."

"You're keeping Zeke?" Sophie said.

"So you can go to Bible study," Boppa said. He wiggled his caterpillar eyebrows.

"Matter of fact, I have him for the rest of the week."

"Coolio!" Zeke crowed.

"He might not be so happy after he spends an afternoon with Miss Odetta," Fiona muttered to Sophie as they climbed into the third seat. She squeezed Sophie's hand. "But I am."

10

Sophie didn't have time to wonder how it had all come about, because the minute she walked into the Bible study room, Dr. Peter gave them red carnations to pin on, and fake cigars and black felt fedora hats. Sophie squealed as she dipped hers over one eye.

"This is swell!" she said.

"What's the deal?" Gill said. She put the fedora on top of her ball cap.

"The deal is, we're doing this Bible study twenties-style, see?" Dr. Peter said. He parked a phony cigar between his molars and talked out the other side of his mouth. "You dolls sit down and shut yer yaps. I'm the boss here, see, and you dames do what I say or else."

Kitty giggled and stuck the carnation behind her ear.

"So yer a tough guy, huh?" Sophie said in her best Goodsy Malone voice.

"Yeah."

"Says you." Sophie chewed on the cigar and gave him a Goodsy glare.

"Yeah, says me. Yer all a buncha lousy disciples, dirty rats in my book, 'cause ya been nabbed for stuffin' yer cake holes with grain on a Sunday." Dr. Peter glowered at all of them from under the brim of his hat. "And the Boss don't like that. It's against the rules, see?"

Kitty giggled again.

"Is he for real?" Maggie said to Darbie.

"That bulge in his jacket ain't his wallet," Darbie said. "He's packin' heat."

"So, what now?" Fiona said.

"What do you have to say for yourselves?" Dr. Peter said.

Sophie smothered a grin. "Get outta town," she said. "That ain't what the law means. I gotta buncha hungry dolls here, see? What am I supposed to do, let 'em starve?"

"Who are you, their mommy?" Dr. Peter said. He stuck his hand inside his jacket. Fiona gave a shrill flapper-girl scream and rolled onto the floor, dragging Darbie with her.

"Huh?" Maggie said.

"Don't get your knickers in a knot, girls," Sophie said. "He's all talk. He ain't gonna shoot us over a coupla lousy grains a wheat."

"It's the principle of the thing!" Dr. Peter said.

"We can't eat your lousy principle," Sophie said. "See, that's the difference between you and me, Mr. Stinky Cigar."

"Oh yeah? How's that?"

"You'd let your own grandmother go hungry over a lousy rule 'cause you ain't got no heart. Me — us — we got heart.

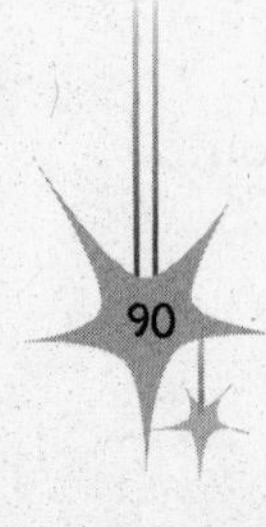

When somebody needs somethin', we do it for 'em; don't matter what day it is."

Dr. Peter's hand went farther into his jacket.

"I'm telling you, he's got a rod in there," Fiona said.

"He'll pump us fulla bullets!" Darbie cried.

"They're kidding," Maggie said to Kitty.

"So lemme ask you this," Dr. Peter said, narrowing his twinkly eyes. "You just gonna forget about Sunday altogether? Treat it like any other lousy day?"

"Says you!" Sophie said. "It's the Sabbath, and we're keepin' it holy. If we gotta do a little work to help somebody, that's still holy, see?"

"Yeah?" Dr. Peter said.

"Well, yeah," Sophie said. "I mean — " Her Goodsy voice faded into a Sophie squeak. "I get it."

Dr. Peter nodded. "Y'know," he said, "I like a smart doll like you."

Then he pulled his "weapon" out of his pocket and sprayed them all with Silly String.

Later, while they were pulling it out of their hair and eating Baby Ruth bars (Dr. Peter said they were invented in the twenties), Sophie was still thinking about the story.

"So the only time you can break a rule is when it would really help somebody to break it," she said. "Right?"

"Tell me some more," Dr. Peter said.

Sophie picked her words carefully. "Like if we had a rule with our friends that we would always help each other when we were in trouble — but one friend wanted somebody to lie to help her, only that really wouldn't help her — we should break the rule."

"Right," Dr. Peter said. "Only you wouldn't really be breaking it, because love and compassion and truth are never against the law."

Sophie could almost see that soaking into everyone's brains.

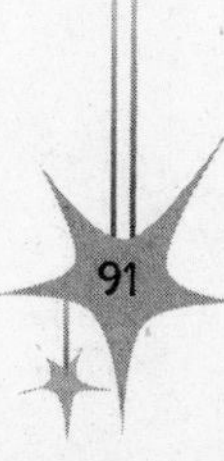

"Another important part of that," Dr. Peter said, "is that the original rule, to be loyal and help each other, still stands. Just like we should always try not to work on Sunday, unless we have to so we can feed somebody who's hungry in some way."

Sophie nodded. It felt like one small knot was starting to come undone.

"You were talking about Willoughby, weren't you?" Fiona said when they were all—except Kitty—in the car with Boppa and Zeke.

"Yeah," Sophie said. "And I think I know what to do to get her back in the Corn Flakes."

"Then tell," Darbie said. "I've been wretched all day missing her."

"And how," Fiona said.

Sophie tried to sit taller. "Even though she thinks we broke the rule, we still have to help her."

"How are we going to help her see that those eighth graders are bad for her?" Fiona said. "She's, like, obsessed."

"We do what Dr. Peter said. We feed her." Sophie shrugged. "You know, like take her a party."

"Right now?" Maggie said.

Fiona snorted. "Like that's going to happen."

There was a cough from the driver's seat. "Why not?" Boppa said. "There's never a better time for a party than right now." He picked up his cell phone and punched a number.

"What's he doing?" Maggie whispered.

Fiona rolled her eyes. "You got me."

Sophie listened, wide-eyed, as Boppa talked to her mother. When they got to Sophie's, Mama was on the couch, ready to act as Take-Willoughby-a-Party coordinator.

She sent Boppa and Zeke to the store for sodas and chips, while Sophie and Maggie foraged in the kitchen for other snacks, with

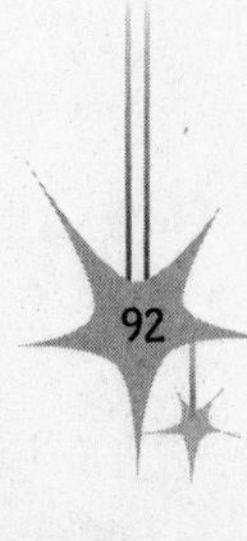

Lacie pulling stuff off the shelves for them so they wouldn't mess up her pantry. Mama sent Fiona and Darbie to Daddy's computer to print up signs that read "We love you, Willoughby" and "We want you back!" At the last minute, before the girls piled back into the Expedition, Sophie grabbed a box of Corn Flakes from the pantry.

When Boppa pulled into Willoughby's driveway, he turned to the girls and said, "You take as long as you want, ladies. I'll wait out here."

"I have to admit that was swell of Boppa," Fiona said as they hauled their party-in-bags up to the front door.

Sophie glanced back at the car where Boppa was watching them in a pool of light from the streetlamp. Later, she wanted to tell him he was no longer on the evil Parent Patrol — he or Mama.

"Yo, Willoughby!" Fiona yelled as she hammered the doorbell. "Open up!"

Sophie heard footsteps on the other side, and then a pause. For a moment she was afraid Willoughby wasn't going to open the door. But then she did, and Darbie and Maggie waved the signs. Willoughby burst into tears.

"Does that mean she wants us to go away?" Maggie said.

"No!" Willoughby cried. "It means I love you!" She pulled them in, still wailing and laughing, and hugged each one of them until Sophie was sure there would be broken ribs.

"I'm sorry — ," Willoughby said.

But Fiona stuffed a potato chip in her mouth. "We know," she said. "Now hush up and let's party."

"I brought you a present," Sophie said. She held up the cereal box.

"Am I still a Corn Flake?" Willoughby said as she hugged it against her.

"Is Al Capone Italian?" Darbie said.

Willoughby sobered. "I don't know — is he?"

"You have missed way too many rehearsals," Fiona said.

Willoughby let out a poodle-shriek, which brought an ear-to-ear smile to Sophie's face. It also brought Willoughby's father down the stairs.

"What's going on, Willoughby?" he said. Sophie could tell the growl wasn't far away.

"The girls came to see me — "

"When you're grounded?" Mr. Wiley's voice rose to dogfight level. "What are you thinking — you can't have friends in here when you're grounded. What's the matter with you?"

"I'm sorry," Willoughby said.

"Sorry doesn't cut it."

"But I — "

It was as if Willoughby's father had forgotten there were four other girls standing there, staring at their toes, rigid as poles. Sophie's stomach was tying itself into a noose when Fiona poked her to say something.

"We should go," Sophie said. Her voice came out small.

Maggie got the door open, and they all shot out of it.

"Bye, ya'll," Willoughby said in a quivery voice.

"Get to your room!" her father said.

The door slammed, shutting away the sight of Willoughby, hugging her Corn Flakes box and cringing. The girls skittered down the steps, but not before Sophie heard a thud and a cry like a wounded poodle.

One look at the other Corn Flakes, and she knew they had heard it too. They stood frozen at the bottom of the steps, until Maggie said, "Let's get out of here."

"Right," Darbie said. "I don't want to hear any more."

But Sophie couldn't move. "What about Willoughby?" she said.

Fiona grabbed Sophie's wrist and pulled her along. "I don't think she gets to party tonight, Soph."

"But what are we going to do?"

Darbie stopped and huddled the girls in with her arms. "I don't think we can do anything. I mean, he's her father."

"He shouldn't hit her," Maggie said.

Fiona's eyes bulged. "You want to go tell *him* that?"

"I didn't know he was a mean dad, did you?" Darbie said.

Sophie could hardly swallow, and the words "I should have known" barely came out.

"Should we tell someone?" Darbie said.

"I thought we said we'd help with parent stuff, not get each other in *more* trouble," Fiona said.

Sophie shook her head. "Dr. Peter said you have to break the rule if it helps somebody, and if we don't — "

"Just stop." Darbie put her hand up. "Maybe we're about to make a holy show out of something that's nothing. We do that sometimes." She pulled the girls in closer. "Why don't we ask Willoughby what happened before we tell any adults?"

"Brilliant," Fiona said. She was nodding harder than she needed to, Sophie thought. "Tomorrow, third period, we ask her."

Sophie looked back at the door. "I know what I heard," she said.

"We're just double-checking, Soph," Fiona said.

Because we don't want to believe it's true, Sophie thought as they hurried toward the Expedition.

"Not a word about this to Boppa yet," Fiona whispered.

Sophie actually didn't say anything at all on the way home or after she got there. She wasn't sure she could speak anyway, not with the knots that were now taking over her throat too. All she could do was close her eyes and imagine the kind eyes and beg Jesus to show her just which rule to follow.

"You do the talking, Soph," Fiona said the next day as she and Darbie hurried along with Sophie to the PE locker room at the beginning of third period to meet Maggie and Willoughby.

"You always say the right things," Darbie said.

All Sophie could think of to say right now was, *Jesus—please help!*

Because it wasn't just about a Film Club project anymore, or parents who wouldn't let them do adult things. It wasn't even about eighth-grade cheerleaders using a seventh-grade girl to get them out of trouble.

Now it was about Willoughby being with a father who growled like a dog—and maybe even hit her—hard enough to make her cry out.

Willoughby wasn't in the locker room when they arrived, and Maggie said Willoughby hadn't waited for her after second period.

"She'll run in here late again," Darbie said. "All in flitters."

"Get ready," Fiona said. "Sophie can ask her while we're changing her clothes."

Willoughby did burst in with only forty-five seconds left until roll call. "The team is ready," Fiona told her.

But as Maggie and Darbie stripped off Willoughby's backpack and jacket, and Sophie and Fiona went after her ankle boots, Willoughby pulled away.

"Ya'll go ahead," she said, flashing them the plastic smile. "I don't want to make you late."

"Corn Flakes don't let any of their own be late, see?" Fiona said, flapper-girl style.

"Shut yer yap and let me have that shirt," Darbie said.

She slid Willoughby's sleeve off her arm. Sophie had to put her hand over her mouth to keep from gasping out loud. Bruises blued Willoughby's skin from shoulder to elbow. From the way Fiona was frozen over the other arm, Sophie was sure she saw the same thing there.

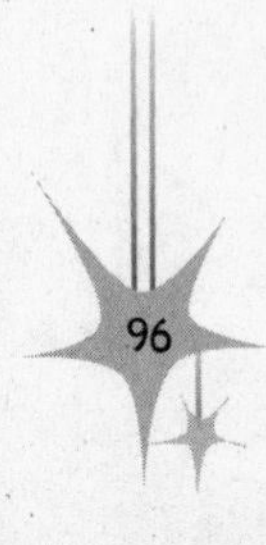

"I can really do this myself," Willoughby said. She turned her back to them and fumbled with her locker combination.

Fiona motioned everyone away with her head and gave Sophie a hard look.

"So," Sophie said in a voice that was over-the-top cheerful, "did you get punished because we came over yesterday? We didn't mean to get you in trouble."

"Not by *my* dad," Willoughby said. Her poodle-shriek came out thin and shrill. "He acts like he's all grouchy and mean sometimes, but he doesn't ever punish us." She twirled around, arms now covered. "He's a cool dad."

"He grounded you," Maggie said.

"For like ten minutes," Willoughby said. "And he apologized after you left."

"You girls that anxious to get detention?" Coach Yates yelled from the end of the locker row.

Willoughby jumped, and Sophie saw the fear-flecks in her eyes. She was the first one out of the locker room, still wearing the phony smile.

"She was lying," Maggie said as the rest of the Corn Flakes hurried out behind her.

"Uh, you think?" Fiona said.

Darbie edged close to Sophie in the roll-call line. "Did you see those bruises?" Sophie felt her shiver. "I'm never going to complain about Aunt Emily and Uncle Patrick again."

"Wiley!" Coach Yates yelled.

Nobody answered.

Coach Yates looked up from her attendance sheet, and for a second, her eyes looked worried. "She was just here. Where is she?"

"Should I answer for her?" Fiona whispered.

Sophie shook her head. It was time to break the rule—the one that said they would handle all their parent problems themselves.

This one, she knew, was way too big, even for the Corn Flakes.

11

At lunch, sandwiches and chips and even Maggie's mother's homemade sopaipillas went uneaten as the Corn Flakes talked in hushed voices. Willoughby wasn't with them, and Maggie said she hadn't shown up for fourth-period math either.

"So none of us have seen her since we dressed out for gym," Fiona said. "It's like she evaporated."

Darbie's eyebrows came together under her red bangs. "For all we know, she's still running around in her PE clothes."

"If she's cutting classes, she's gonna be in so much trouble with her dad." Maggie's words sounded even heavier than usual. They seemed to press everyone deeper into worry.

"We have to tell a grown-up," Sophie said. "We know her dad's hurting her—we heard—we saw the bruises—and you remember that other time when we were helping her change and she said she fell over the coffee table? I bet—"

"She didn't say he hit her, though," Fiona said.

They all stared at her.

Fiona rolled her eyes. "Okay, so she didn't have to. But what if we tell, and they put her in some foster home?"

There was a stunned silence, the kind of scary quiet that usually sent Sophie straight to Goodsy Malone's world. But somehow she knew even Goodsy didn't have an answer. And she didn't even have to close her eyes to see who did.

"I say we stick with our Code," Fiona said. "Or we're just going to make things worse."

"I say we stick with the Code too," Sophie said. "Only the Code says we always help when somebody's in trouble. The Jesus kind of help. Not lying and hiding stuff."

Fiona sat back and folded her arms. "If we're just going to call the police or something, no way."

"No," Sophie said. "First we tell Willoughby what we're going to do, and then we tell a grown-up we can trust."

"Like Dr. Peter," Darbie said.

Sophie wanted to hug her.

"How are we going to tell Willoughby if we can't even find her?" Maggie said as she dumped her untouched lunch into the garbage can.

"We keep looking until we do," Sophie said. She stuck out her pinky finger.

"Corn Flake promise," Darbie said.

Maggie hooked on.

Finally, Fiona did too. "I hate this," she said. "I wish our biggest problem was still how to make a kidnapping scene so every parent in America won't yell."

"And how," Sophie said. "I wish we could all just be kids."

She felt strangely old all afternoon as she took every possible chance to find Willoughby. She even got a restroom pass from grouchy Coach Yates so she could search the stalls. When she came back, disappointed, Coach Yates met her at the door.

"How long does it take to use the restroom, LaCroix?" she said.

Sophie groped for a comeback, but she only felt herself crumpling.

"Sorry," she said, "I was looking for Willoughby." Coach Yates' eyes sprang open, enough for Sophie to add, "Do you know where she is?"

"No, I don't know where she is. If you kids can't get yourselves to class, what am I supposed to do about it?"

I don't know, Sophie thought. *Care, maybe?*

Coach Yates pressed her lips together until they turned white. "I apologize, LaCroix," she said. "I'm just concerned about — a student. It's been bugging me for two weeks. You're a good kid — I shouldn't take it out on you."

Sophie hoped her mouth wasn't hanging completely open.

"Go on back inside," Coach said. "And let me know if you hear from Wiley, okay? She's a good kid too."

Her dad doesn't think so!

Sophie put her hand up to her mouth to make sure she hadn't said it out loud, but her lips were closed.

We have to find Willoughby soon, she thought, *or I really* am *going to tell somebody.*

By the next morning, it truly seemed, as Fiona said, Willoughby had evaporated. She hadn't answered Sophie's emails — or anyone else's, it turned out — and there had been no answer on her house phone or her cell phone. Sophie had avoided both Mama and Daddy, and she had imagined Jesus until she fell asleep, partly so she *wouldn't* imagine what might be happening to Willoughby at her house.

Nobody — Corn Flakes or Fruit Loops — had any news about her first period — nobody except Mrs. Clayton. She called Sophie out into the hall right after the bell rang.

"Willoughby Wiley is coming before the Round Table today at lunch," she said.

"Willoughby?" Sophie said. "She's here?"

"In Mr. Bentley's office, I assume." Mrs. Clayton's bullet eyes weren't firing. "She cut four of her classes yesterday. The librarian found her hiding out in the reference section."

Sophie didn't know whether to shout, "Yes!" or just plain cry. Willoughby was really in trouble now. And when her dad found out —

"Usually they would just give a student in-school suspension for that," Mrs. Clayton said. "But Mr. Bentley feels there's something else going on, and I agree. He would rather see the Round Table work with her. Maybe Coach Nanini."

Sophie did say "Yes!" then.

But Mrs. Clayton had more. "There's a problem, though," she said. "With you."

"Me?"

"Willoughby informed me during our preliminary meeting before school this morning that maybe you shouldn't be on the council today because you 'fixed' the outcome for two of her friends, and you might do the same for her. She doesn't want that."

Sophie could only stare at her.

"I'm not assuming that what she says is true," Mrs. Clayton said. "In fact, I'm inclined to believe it isn't. But the fact is that you and Willoughby are very close, and I'm not sure you could be completely objective. She does have a point there."

Sophie's mind was spinning like a bicycle wheel, but she managed to poke a stick in the spokes long enough to say, "But nobody knows Willoughby better than I do! I could really help her!"

Mrs. Clayton shook her head of cemented hair. "She may need your help in other ways, but I think you ought to sit this one out, Sophie."

How am I supposed to see justice done? thought Goodsy Malone as she scraped her chair up to her desk, when I can't even be in the courtroom? She slumped in her seat. I gotta talk to her, see? I gotta tell her we need to rat on her old man, but it's for her own good.

Goodsy pulled the rod from her shoulder holster and let it thud to the top of the desk. Why try to fight violence on the streets if people's homes weren't even safe for them?

Someone across the room coughed. Goodsy looked up—

Fiona nodded toward Sophie's desktop. Her hairbrush was lying where she'd dropped it, and everyone else had their faces in their lit books. Sophie pulled hers out, but all she could see on the pages was Willoughby with fear-flecks in her eyes.

Why did she tell Mrs. Clayton about me helping Victoria and Ginger? she thought. *It's like she doesn't want me there.*

But why?

Sophie asked herself that question all through PE and math class. It was the only thing she could talk about at lunch.

"I don't get it either," Fiona said. "She knows you're the fairest person in life."

"She's making a bags of it," Darbie said. "Poor thing."

"Here comes Jimmy," Maggie said. She shook her head soberly. "It didn't go so good."

Jimmy did look as if he'd rather be delivering a baby than the news he obviously had for them.

"Just tell me fast," Sophie said. "I can't stand it any longer."

Jimmy shoved his hands into his pockets. "She's not getting ISS, so nothing will go on her record. We gave her Campus Commission."

"After school?" Fiona said.

Jimmy nodded.

"Her dad's gonna be mad," Maggie said. "Way mad."

"Mad?" Darbie said. "He'll be furious."

"It's not like it's detention," Jimmy said.

"Her father won't get that," Sophie said.

"Yeah, but—" Jimmy hunched his shoulders as if Sophie might smack him. "You would have voted the same way if you'd been there."

Sophie had to nod. And then something shifted in her mind.

"That's why Willoughby didn't want me there," she said. "She knew I would vote that way because it's fair. It's what I did for those eighth graders the second time."

"She did look kinda surprised when Hannah suggested it and Oliver agreed with her." Jimmy shrugged. "I guess she thought they wouldn't."

Sophie shot up from the table. "So where is she now?"

"Going to class, I guess."

"We're there," Fiona said.

For the second day in a row, the Corn Flakes tossed their uneaten lunches into the trash. Sophie led them at a dead run to Miss Imes' classroom, but even ten seconds before the bell rang, when Darbie, Fiona, and Sophie had to get to science, there was still no Willoughby.

"Maybe Mrs. Clayton kept her after the meeting," Miss Imes said. "Surely she wouldn't cut class again after we just went easy on her."

"Willoughby doesn't see it that way," Fiona said as they tore for the science room.

"Neither does her father," Darbie said.

Sophie didn't say anything. She was too busy asking herself why they hadn't told an adult about Willoughby's father already. She had an old thought, one she hadn't had in several weeks.

I wish I could talk to Mama and Daddy about it right now.

Two days ago it would have seemed like a ridiculous idea. But today, it almost didn't matter that Daddy still thought she was a little girl. Right now she felt like one — a little girl with too many adult things in her head.

"You okay, Sophie?"

Sophie looked up to see Mr. Stires standing beside her desk. The rest of the class was gathered in small groups.

"I'm sorry," Sophie said. "I'll go be in Fiona's group."

"I told her to go on without you." Mr. Stires sat in the desk beside hers. His always-cheerful face looked confused, as if he didn't know how to be anything but happy.

"I heard about Willoughby," he said. "I don't understand it. Do you?"

"Sort of," Sophie said.

"You want to tell me?"

Sophie caught her breath. Mr. Stires probably never would have appeared on a list of adults she would talk to about a problem. But here he was, right at the moment when she needed a grown-up.

"I don't know why Willoughby cut her classes yesterday," Sophie said. "All I know is that she's afraid of her father. He's kind of — mean to her. Actually — really mean."

There. It was out. Mr. Stires wasn't Daddy or Dr. Peter, but at least —

"It makes sense now." Mr. Stires rubbed his fingers across his toothbrush mustache. "When Mr. Wiley called me and said your kidnapping scene was far too dark for seventh graders, he was angry. Too angry for the situation — "

Mr. Stires stopped suddenly, as if he'd said too much. It was enough for Sophie — enough to make her feel even smaller than she already was.

I just automatically thought it was Daddy, she thought. *I should have known.* Daddy wasn't Mr. Wiley, not even close.

"Do you think I could have a pass to the office?" Sophie said. "I want to call my dad."

Daddy answered his office phone on the first ring. Before Sophie could even get out "Hi, Daddy" all the way, he said, "What's wrong, Baby Girl? You okay?"

Sophie started to cry. She couldn't stop the whole time she was telling Daddy about Willoughby and her father, and what might happen now.

Daddy listened without interrupting. When she was through, there was such a long pause Sophie thought they had been disconnected.

"Daddy?" she said.

"Yeah, Baby Girl," he said. "I'm here. I'm just thinking." He pushed out some air. "Okay, here's what we'll do. You go on back to class and do your best to get through the rest of the day. I'll take care of this."

Sophie didn't even ask him what he was going to do. What *she* had to do was done, and she was suddenly very tired.

This is backwards from the way we were gonna do it, she thought as she took the hall back to the science room. *But I still need to tell Willoughby.*

Mrs. Clayton had to be finished with her by now, and Willoughby would be in Life Skills sixth period.

There was barely time before the end of science to join Fiona, Darbie, Vincent, and Jimmy in their group and fill them in on her phone call to Daddy. Even Fiona looked relieved. The boys were white-faced.

"So," Fiona said, "now we find Willoughby."

"We'll run interference for you," Vincent said. He and Jimmy cleared a people-free path in the hall so Sophie could be the first one at Coach Yates' door when kids started filing in.

But when Maggie arrived, she shook her head.

"She wasn't in math," she said.

"Are you talking about Willoughby?"

Sophie whirled around to face Cassie Corn Pop. She pushed her dislike out of the way and said, "Yes, I'm talking about Willoughby. Do you know something?" *Something that might actually be true?* Sophie wanted to add. "Just — do you know where she is?"

"I know where she isn't," Cassie said. By now Julia was at her side, looking curious. Cassie was apparently ready to take her moment in Julia's spotlight. It was all Sophie could do not to grab her and shake her.

"*Where?*" Sophie said instead. She didn't care that her voice was squeaking out of control.

Cassie glanced at Julia as if to make sure she was paying attention before she brought her face close to Sophie's and said, "She's not hiding out here at school anymore. I just saw her running across the parking lot." Julia gasped, and Cassie's eyes took on a shine. "Girl," she said, "she's out of here."

12

"Did I just hear what I think I heard?" Fiona said.

Sophie turned from watching Julia and Cassie disappear into the classroom, Cassie still basking in Julia's impressed gaze. "Did you think you heard that Willoughby just left school?" she said.

"Yeah."

"Then you did."

"Well, let's go find her then," Darbie said. "Why are we foostering about?"

"We definitely have to get to her before somebody from the school does." Fiona glanced at her watch. "How far do you think she'll get in forty-five minutes?"

"No," Sophie said.

"No what?" Fiona said.

"No, we can't just look for her ourselves. We have to tell an adult that she left school."

Fiona grabbed Sophie's arm and hauled her into the classroom. "You'll get her in more trouble, and it won't be just Campus Commission this time," she said through her teeth.

"And her father—," Darbie said.

But Sophie pulled away. "She's going to be in a worse kind of trouble if somebody doesn't stop her right this minute. We have to tell somebody who can do that."

With Fiona and Darbie still protesting behind her, Sophie went to Coach Yates, who had her whistle to her lips, ready to blow the class into silence. One look at Sophie's face, and she had Sophie out in the hall.

The story came out easier than it had with Daddy, as Sophie raced to the part where Willoughby was seen running from the schoolyard. For a few seconds, Coach Yates closed her eyes.

"I'm not surprised," she said. "I've been trying to get Willoughby to tell me this for weeks."

Sophie wondered if Willoughby was the student Coach Yates had said she was concerned about, the one who was making her grumpy. She could almost see Willoughby flashing a too-cheerful smile the day Coach Yates took her aside. There was no way Willoughby was telling anybody, even her best friends.

"All right," Coach Yates said. "I'll get word to the office. You did the right thing, LaCroix. I said you were a good kid."

"You said Willoughby was a good kid too," Sophie said.

"She is." Coach Yates opened the door for Sophie. "That's why we have to get her some help."

Sophie tried to explain that to Maggie and Fiona and Darbie.

"Dr. Peter told us really helping is never against the rules," she said, "even the rules we make up ourselves. Jesus would do this."

"We're not Jesus," Fiona said stubbornly.

Darbie shook her head, scattering her bangs. "Jesus would go look for her."

"So why can't we look too?"

They stared at Maggie.

"Mags is right," Sophie said. "We can still look for her. We just shouldn't be the *only* ones."

Fiona's face unclouded slightly. "Where do we start?"

They mapped out a plan. As soon as the last bell rang, Sophie sprinted straight to the eighth-grade locker area. If anybody looked at her like she was an intruder, she didn't notice. She had eyes only for Ginger and Victoria. She'd heard them say they wouldn't hang out with Willoughby anymore, but she had to try everything.

The moment they appeared, Sophie was on them.

"Did you talk to Willoughby today?" she said.

The two girls looked at each other and had one of those unspoken best-friends conversations with their eyes. Sophie was surprised to see that they didn't seem to exactly agree.

"No," Victoria said. "Look, Stephi — we haven't talked to her in, like, a week, okay?" She gave her blonde-over-blonde hair a toss and swept away, and what seemed like half the boys in the eighth grade followed her.

Ginger didn't. She spoke low and fast.

"Tell anybody I told you this, and I'll ruin your dating life forever," she said. "I talked to Willoughby. She was hysterical when she got Campus Commission for skipping, and I felt responsible because we showed her where to hide out when she wanted to cut class." She raked a hand through her elfin-hair. "I guess we forgot to tell her how not to get caught. Anyway, she told me today she was going to some neighbor's just to get her head straight. I told her to pack

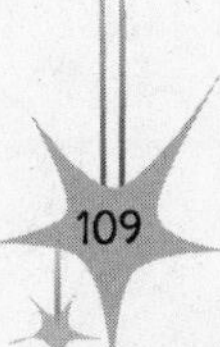

a couple of changes of clothes. Getting *her* head straight was going to take some time."

"*Gin*—ger!" Victoria called from the lockers. Before Sophie could ask another question, Ginger was gone.

I don't care about my "dating life" anyway, Sophie thought as she rushed off to tell her Corn Flakes. *EWWW!*

"Willoughby's neighborhood is Kitty's neighborhood," Fiona said when Sophie told them.

"You don't think she would try to hide out at Kitty's?" Darbie said.

"No," Fiona said. "But if we go there, we might see her."

Fiona called Boppa for a ride. Darbie went in search of the Lucky Charms, and Maggie phoned Kitty to tell her they were coming. Sophie prayed, and by the time they piled into the Expedition, she had a brilliant idea to share.

"Don't you want to wait 'til we get there to tell us?" Fiona said, shifting her eyes significantly toward Boppa.

"No," Sophie said, "'cause Boppa can help."

Although Fiona looked ready to pull out Sophie's nose hairs when they arrived at Kitty's, Boppa was checked out on the plan, complete with Kitty's phone number programmed into his cell phone.

"I'll call the minute I see her," he said, and he pulled off in the Expedition to patrol the streets for Willoughby.

The Charms set up for the kidnapping scene in Kitty's front yard while the Flakes explained to Kitty why they were having a film rehearsal at the very moment that Willoughby was missing.

"She's not going to let us find *her*," Fiona said. "So we have to let her find *us*."

Sophie gave a satisfied sigh. Fiona was finally getting it.

Vincent yelled that he was ready with the camera, and everyone got into position. Kitty had the phone in her lap in the wheelchair.

"Action!" Vincent called out.

Al Capone/Jimmy and his right-hand man, Thug Nathan, barely had time to sneak up behind poor little sick Bitsy O'Banyon when the phone rang. Sophie leaped out of the bushes and leaned in as Kitty held the receiver away from her ear.

"She's headed down Valmoore Drive," Boppa said. "She hasn't seen me yet. I'm keeping my distance. She's right around the corner from you."

"Now!" Sophie said between her teeth.

Vincent abandoned the camera. He, Jimmy, and Nathan tore off like a herd of giraffes. Maggie and Darbie helped Kitty out of the wheelchair so she could go inside with the phone. She'd watch for her cue with her mom through the window. Sophie saw Kitty clinging to her before they closed the drapes almost all the way.

Sophie's job was to pray again: *Please let this work. We're really trying to play by your rules now.*

"Here they come!" Fiona said from her stakeout by the mailbox. She ran back to the Corn Flakes just as the Lucky Charms rounded the corner. Jimmy had Willoughby over his shoulder, screaming like a whole litter of poodle puppies. Nathan was carrying a suitcase.

Does she believe everything those eighth graders tell her? Sophie thought.

"Can you get this dame to shut up?" Jimmy/Al Capone said as he deposited Willoughby in front of Darbie and Fiona, the flapper girls. Sophie/Goodsy and Maggie/Loyal Sidekick Malloy stood apart and waited for their cue.

"Shut your cake hole and nobody'll get hurt," Fiona/Flapper Fran said to Willoughby.

"What are you doing?" Willoughby said. Her eyes were frantic as she looked over her shoulder and back at them, and then over her shoulder again.

"Making you look like somethin', for one thing," said Darbie/Soozy Floozy. "Get that jacket off her. Where's the fur coat?"

Fiona produced the oversize fake-fur coat Maggie's mom had made.

Make the change fast, Sophie thought. *It's cold out here.*

Willoughby was already shivering before Fiona and Darbie pulled her jean jacket off. When Nathan let out a long whistle at the sight of her black and blue arms, she began to shake like a wet dog.

"Let me go!" she screamed. "I don't want to rehearse. I have to go!"

Somehow they got the fur coat on her, but not before Sophie saw there were new bruises that hadn't been there the day before.

Hurry up, you guys, she wanted to call to the Capone gang. *Get her in the chair.*

"We can't let you go, see?" Jimmy/Capone said. "Because we gotta kidnap you."

"I don't have time!" Willoughby cried.

"Nobody has 'time' to be kidnapped, sister," Fiona/Flapper Fran said. She nodded toward the chair. Willoughby followed with her eyes and screamed louder, "No! Let go of me!"

Jimmy/Capone and Thug Nathan looked like they wanted to let her go, especially when Willoughby began to kick. But Vincent helped them get her into Kitty's wheelchair. Fiona and Darbie were ready with Kitty's mother's clothesline.

"Not too tight," Jimmy said in his own voice as they wrapped the line around Willoughby and the chair. "Her arms — "

"My arms are *fine*!" Willoughby screamed. "Now would you just get me out of this thing — I can't rehearse today!"

Sophie took her cue, only she didn't go to Willoughby as Goodsy Malone. It was Sophie herself who knelt down in front

of the wheelchair and took both of Willoughby's hands. Willoughby tried, but she couldn't pull away.

"We're not rehearsing," Sophie said. "This is real life."

"Your life," Fiona put in.

"Please, Sophie," Willoughby said. Her words were choking out in sobs. "You don't understand — I have to get away!"

"We do understand," Sophie said.

"We know about your dad," Darbie said.

Willoughby froze. "What do you know? There's nothing to know — " her voice broke. "He's a good dad."

"Even a good dad makes mistakes sometimes."

Sophie had never been so happy to hear her father's voice. When she saw Dr. Peter walking up with him, she knew it was more than Kitty and her mom making that phone call at the right time. This was a Jesus answer.

"Why don't you all come inside for hot chocolate?" Mrs. Munford called from the porch. "You'll catch your death of pneumonia out there."

Nobody rolled their eyes. In fact, all the kids ran to her like lost-and-found four-year-olds. Except Sophie, who was wrapped around Daddy's leg.

"Let's talk, Willoughby," Dr. Peter said when he had untied her.

Willoughby looked at Sophie, tears glistening on her cheeks as if they were freezing. "Why did you tell on my dad?" she said.

"Because she's your friend," Dr. Peter said before Sophie could get her mouth open. She made a note in her head to hug him for that later. "She knew you were hurting, and she wanted you to get help. That's a holy thing."

"But my dad's gonna get in trouble!"

Who cares? Sophie wanted to shout at her. *He's mean to you. He SHOULD get in trouble! Why—*

Daddy tightened his grip on Sophie's shoulder. And then Sophie knew, and she empathized like no other. Mr. Wiley was Willoughby's dad, no matter what. If Sophie hadn't had her own dad holding her up at this very moment, she wasn't sure she could even stand.

"Your dad's a single parent," Dr. Peter said to Willoughby. "That's a big, scary job, and sometimes the stress gets to him, I'm sure. But there's help for that, Willoughby, not trouble. You want things to be better with him?"

"They used to be!" Willoughby said. "He used to be a cool dad. Sometimes he still is — " She threw up her hands as if all the confusing thoughts were in them, and she couldn't hold them any longer. Then she sank against Dr. Peter's chest.

"It's okay, little friend," Dr. Peter said. "We'll get that cool dad back again."

Boppa took the rest of the kids to their houses. Sophie noticed that when they pulled away in the Expedition, Fiona was in the front seat talking away to him.

But in the truck with Daddy, Sophie had so many things she wanted to say, none of them would come out. When they pulled into the driveway at home, Daddy kept the engine running and the heater blasting.

"I'm proud of you, Baby Girl," he said. Then he shook his head. "You're not a baby girl anymore, though, that's obvious. You're growing up right before my eyes."

It did come out then. "I'm not grown yet," Sophie said. "I thought I was, but I wasn't — not like Lacie or you or Mama — or even Goodsy Malone — I tried to be, but I'm so confused about what 'grown-up' even is — and sometimes I don't know which rules to follow — but I'm really trying to figure it out, Daddy — really."

Daddy's mouth was twitching, but in the light from the lamp in the yard, Sophie could see a wet shine in his eyes.

"You know what a real grown-up is, Soph?" he said.

Sophie shook her head.

"A grown-up is a person who knows what she can't handle and turns it over to somebody who can — but she also knows what she knows and she doesn't let anybody else take that away from her." He reached a big hand over and squeezed her tiny shoulder. "I want you to teach our new baby girl that when she gets old enough."

"For real?" Sophie said.

"Who could she want more for a friend than you?" Sophie could see him swallowing. "*I* sure want you for my friend."

"Your friend?" Sophie said.

"I'm still your dad, Soph. I have to steer you right when you start flying off to places I don't think you're ready to go yet." His face went soft. "But I also hope you can trust me as a friend when you've got trouble."

It was Sophie's turn to swallow. "But sometimes you don't get it, Daddy," she said.

"No, I don't," Daddy said. "And I'm going to work on that. I think it's time I let you fly just a little bit — " He put up his hand. "Not too far — just a little."

Sophie felt her stomach start to untie, but still —

"What does that mean?" she said.

"That means I bought myself a new laptop and a new desktop computer today."

"Huh?" Sophie said. *Talk about flying off into weird places —*

"And *that* means my old laptop is in Lacie's room at this moment as we speak, and my old desktop is on your desk."

"Says you!" Sophie cried.

"Yeah, says me." Daddy locked his fingers and stretched out his arms. "Incredible father that I am." He grinned. "Now, there are going to be rules for the Internet — "

Sophie nodded happily. Rules were fine. In fact, rules were the cat's pajamas.

She closed her eyes, and there were the kind eyes. And the best rules were right there in them.

Glossary

bee's knees (beez kneez) the way someone from the 1920s said "that's really cool"

bushwa (boosh-wah) complete nonsense

cat's pajamas (CATS puh-jam-uhs) when something's really impressive; you could also say it's the "cat's meow"

chemotherapy (key-mo-THER-a-pee) really strong chemicals that are used as a treatment for cancer

eejit (eeg-it) the way someone from Ireland might say "idiot"

empathize (EM-puh-thize) feeling for someone and putting yourself in their place, because you went through the same thing in the past

flappers (FLA-purs) girls from the 1920s who cut their hair short and wore really cool hats and short skirts (at least short for that time!); parents and other adults were shocked because they didn't act like "proper young ladies"

Flitters (FLI-turs) a feeling you get when you're really excited, like when your body gets all shaky because you're waiting for something to happen

foostering about (foo-stur-ing a-bout) an Irish way of saying "stop wasting time"

gadzooks (ghad-zooks) an exclamation of surprise, especially when something is a little different from what you expected

giving cheek (ghiv-ing cheek) talking back to someone, or acting a little snotty

leukemia (loo-KEY-me-uh) a type of cancer; it attacks your healthy blood cells, especially in your bone marrow, so that you become very sick

make a bags of (mayk a bags of) do a poor job at, or screw things up

nontraditional (non-trah-dish-un-al) something that doesn't follow the way you normally do things

pussyfoot around (pussy-foot uh-rownd) carefully avoiding something; talking about everything but the real issue when someone brings it up

rod (rhod) a slang term for a gun

says you (sez you) a statement of disbelief; telling someone that just because they said it doesn't make it true

scintillating (SIN-tuh-late-ing) something that is really fun, interesting, and even exciting

sumptuous (SUMP-shoe-us) really impressive and over the top

sympathize (sim-pah-thize) feeling sad and concerned for someone when bad things happen

telly (tel-lee) a shortened word for television

up to ninety (up too nine-tea) so incredibly angry, your blood is almost ready to boil, and you're ready to explode on someone

wretched (ret-chid) really upset and concerned about something or someone

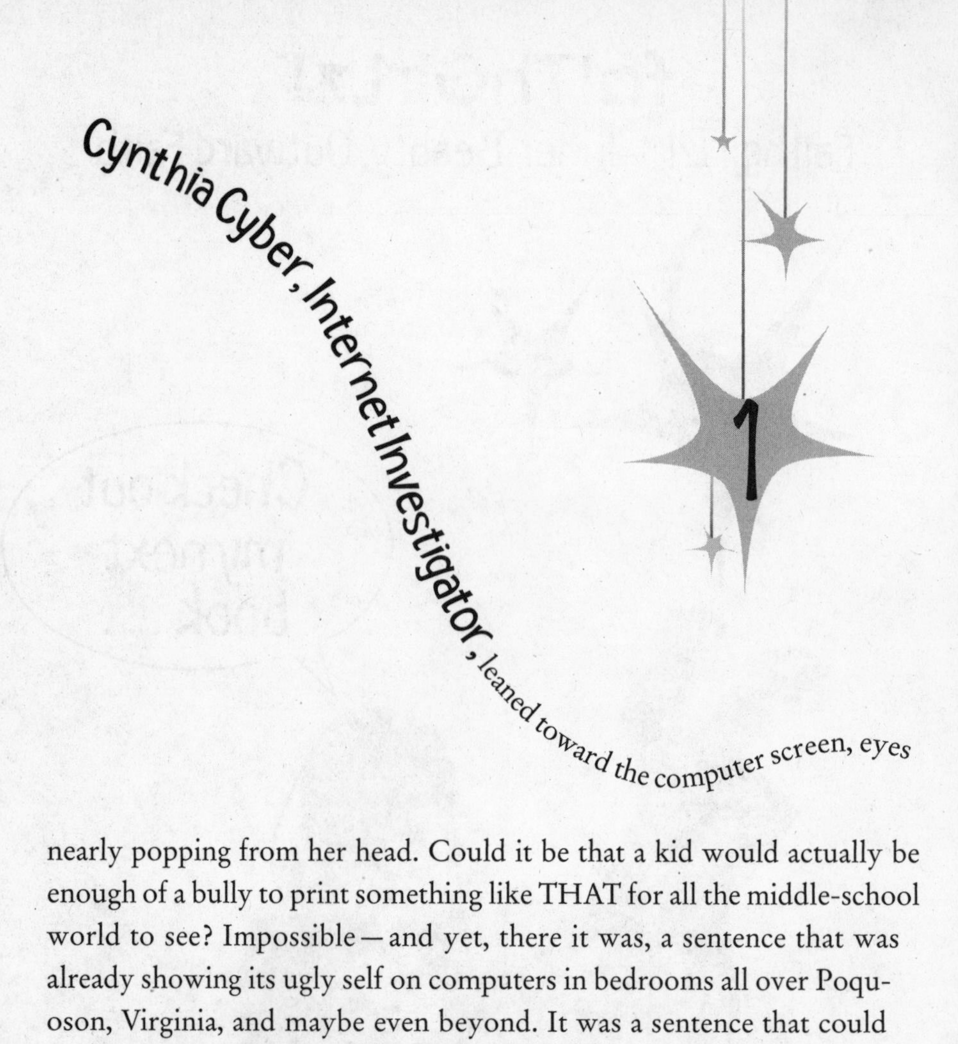

1

Cynthia Cyber, Internet Investigator, leaned toward the computer screen, eyes nearly popping from her head. Could it be that a kid would actually be enough of a bully to print something like THAT for all the middle-school world to see? Impossible — and yet, there it was, a sentence that was already showing its ugly self on computers in bedrooms all over Poquoson, Virginia, and maybe even beyond. It was a sentence that could ravage the social life of its seventh-grade victim before she even checked her email.

"I cannot allow it!" Cynthia Cyber, Internet Investigator, cried. She lunged for the keyboard, fingers already flying —

"It's a seven-passenger van, Little Bit," said a voice from the driver's seat. "You don't have to sit in Jimmy's lap."

Sophie LaCroix jolted back from Sophie-world at several megahertz per second — or something like that. She found herself staring right into Jimmy Wythe's swimming-pool-blue eyes. She had no choice. She really was in his lap.

A round, red spot had formed at the top of each of Jimmy's cheekbones. Sophie was sure her entire face was that color.

"Do you want to sit on this side?" Jimmy said as Sophie scrambled her tiny-for-a-twelve-year-old body back into her own seat. "We could trade."

"I don't think that's what she had in mind." Hannah turned around from the van's middle seat in front of them, blinking her eyes against her contact lenses practically at the speed of sound. She was Sophie's inspiration to keep wearing glasses. "Personally, I think seventh grade's a little young to be dating. I know I'm only a year older, but — "

Mrs. Clayton didn't turn around in the front seat, but her trumpet voice blared its way back to them just fine. "There is actually a world of difference between seventh graders and eighth graders."

Yeah, Sophie thought, fanning her still-red face with a folder. Eighth graders think it's all about the boy-girl thing. I am SO not dating Jimmy Wythe. Or anybody else! EWWW. She scooted a couple of inches farther away from Jimmy.

It wasn't that Jimmy wasn't a whole lot more decent than most of the boys at Great Marsh Middle School. He was one of the three guys who made films with Sophie and her friends. They didn't make disgusting noises with their armpits and burp the alphabet in the cafeteria — like some other boys she knew. But date him — or anybody else?

I do not BELIEVE so! Sophie screamed in her head

"So, are you guys going out or what?" Hannah said.

"Not that it's any of your business." Oliver, the eighth grader next to her, gave one of the rubber bands on his braces a snap

with his finger. Why, Sophie wondered, did boys have to do stuff like that?

"Oh, come on, dish, Little Bit," Coach Nanini said from behind the wheel. He grinned at Sophie in the rearview mirror in that way that always made Sophie think of a big happy gorilla with no hair. She liked to think of him as Coach Virile.

She had to grin back at him.

"We're not going out," Jimmy said. The red spots still punctuated his cheekbones. "We're just, like, friends."

Mrs. Clayton did turn around this time, although her helmet of too-blonde hair didn't move at all. "That's very noble of you, Jimmy, to get Sophie out of the hot seat like that. You're a gentleman."

"Ooh, Mrs. C," Coach Virile said, still grinning. "Don't you know that's the kiss of death for the adolescent male?"

"It's okay," Jimmy said. He pulled his big-from-doing-gymnastics shoulders all the way up to his now-very-red ears. "It's what my dad's teaching me to be."

"Bravo," Mrs. Clayton said. "I'd like to bring him in and have him train the entire male population of the school."

Coach Virile's voice went up even higher than it usually did, which was pretty squeaky for a guy whose beefy arms stuck out from both sides of the driver's seat. "I thought I was doing that, Mrs. C."

"I wish you'd step it up a little," she said.

Sophie glanced sideways at Jimmy, who was currently ducking his head of short-cropped, sun-blond hair. I guess he is kind of a gentleman, Sophie thought. She had never heard him imitate her high-pitched voice like those Fruit Loop boys did, or seen him knock some girl's pencil off her desk just to be obnoxious. And somehow he managed to be pretty nice and still cool at the same time. The Corn Pops definitely thought so. The we-have-everything girls were always chasing after him.

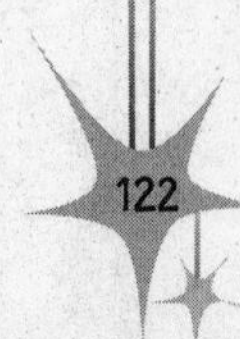

“So if you’re not going out,” Hannah said, “why were you in his lap?”

She was turned all the way around now, arms resting on the back of her seat as if she were going to spend the rest of the trip from Richmond exploring the topic. Oliver groaned.

“Inquiring minds want to know,” Hannah said.

NOSY minds, you mean, Sophie thought. But she sighed and said, “I wasn’t really sitting in his lap. Well, I was, only that wasn’t my plan. I didn’t even know I was doing it, because I was being — well, somebody else — and Jimmy’s window was a computer screen — all our stuff’s piled up and blocking my window so I couldn’t use it — anyway, it all started with the conference. I really got into it.”

Coach Virile laughed, spattering the windshield. “We can always count on you to be honest, Little Bit.”

“Let me get this straight,” said Oliver. “You were pretending to be, like, some imaginary person?”

“More like a character for our next film.”

Jimmy, still blotchy, nodded. “For Film Club. Sophie always comes up with the main character.”

“I play around with it some before I tell the whole group,” Sophie said. “I try not to get too carried away with it in school.” She didn’t add that if she got in trouble for daydreaming, her father would take away her movie camera.

“Ya think?” Hannah said. She put on her serious face. “A little advice: don’t tell that to a whole lot of people at Great Marsh. You’d be committing social suicide.”

“Especially don’t let it get out on the Internet,” Oliver said. “Everybody’ll think you’re weird.”

“I am weird,” Sophie said. “Well, unique. Who isn’t?”